The Return of the Black Witch

Book Two: The Moleskin Cap

M. R. Williamson

WolfSinger Publications ⟨ Security, Colorado

Cover Art copyright 2022 © Tammy LouAnn Williamson Barr
Cover Layout by Carol Hightshoe

ISBN 978-1-944637-11-8

Printed and bound in the United States of America

Table of Contents

Introduction

Three years have passed since the Black Witch, Ethrel Ibenus, was vanquished by the Green Witch Pareen Willingham. Ethrel's familiar, the wolf Seleene, disappeared into the forests that day and out of everyone's mind…save one. Over time, she was almost forgotten. True to form, most of the remaining Dwarves remained aloof, seldom visiting Professor Martin in the forest where the prying eyes of men remained few. Billy Bo Bumpus and his daughter, Entwhistle remained the exception to that rule, however. Visiting at the Professor's home, usually once a week, they kept a strong friendship with both the Professor and his granddaughter, Helen Durkin. True to what Helen had hinted, she chose not to return to her father in London. He seemed too cold and distant.

Pareen Willingham chose to remain close to the Dwarves of Leachenwood. With their help, she was able to reclaim the cottage of her childhood and watch after those who lived in the forests, both Dwarf, human, and animal alike. She constantly drew comfort by being close to the half-Dwarf Long Barr, still held within the Tree of Sorrows by the Black Witch's spell. But, now, normality was about to change once more and allow their different worlds to overlap in a most unexpected way.

Part 1
The Outcast

The half-Dwarf Donder Franks sat nestled inside the branches of an old spruce, listening to the moisture dripping from the trees to the leaves of the forest floor. An early-morning April rain had gifted the wood with just enough moisture to quiet the crackle of the dry leaves from the hunter's approach. Hunger gnawed at the halfling's stomach like a cramp that refused to be rubbed out. A well-used game trail was only a weak toss away from him, but for some reason, nothing was using it this morning. Just as puzzling, even the birds were refusing their normal, spring-like chatter.

Then, hearing a slight rustle in the scrub on the far side of the trail, he quickly put arrow to bow. Fumbling to position it to the string, he watched intently.

Please…not another hare. If it's another rabbit, I'll eat tree bark, he thought almost aloud.

But another noise came to his ears—the soft crunch of dry spruce needles. Donder didn't see the old tree move, but he did, feel the moisture as it fell on his jacket. He slowly turned to check both sides. But the spruce was too thick and he could see not a thing. And worse—the pain in his stomach was back again, causing him to grimace and rub his abdomen. His stomach growled, sounding much like an angry old hound. Sensitive ears caught the sound causing a slight movement beneath a young fir tree.

Good…good.

Seeing dark brown or perhaps blackish fur, he gradually raised his bow and sighted down the arrow toward the spot in the evergreen's shadow.

What part of the animal am I seeing? It's the size of, perhaps, a young deer. But I've never seen a deer with black and tan fur like—

The halfling's thought was cut short by the feel of cold steel just under his chin. His eyes grew big as he let the tension off the bow.

"All right," he managed weakly. "You've got my attention."

But his words drew no comment. Instead, his possible 'deer'

got up, looked toward where Donder was sitting, and then trotted down the game trail and out of sight.

"What the devil kind of dog is that?" he asked, still feeling the cold steel beneath his chin.

"Thank you very much," came the soft, girlish reply, but the knife remained. "I've been trying for six months to gain the trust of that creature and just when I get close, up pops another fool trying to shoot her."

"I'm hungry. Would you mind removing the knife?"

Donder watched the polished blade slide from his throat and pass so close to his left ear it made it twitch. Moving slowly, he turned to see a small, brown-headed dwarf of twenty or so. Her smile was warm, but the knife point was still against his side.

"Wow," he said weakly as she pushed by him through the old spruce. "I never heard you enter the tree."

She paused, two steps in front of him and turned slowly. "Not much of a hunter are you," she said.

"Well…" Donder eased out of the branches and stood up brushing his pants off. "I'm a real terror on rabbits."

"Really?" A slight smile started to form on the little Dwarf's face. "Where do you live?"

Donder straightened up, looking down at her. "A little bit of everywhere really. What kind of dog was that? It was bigger than a hound but looked to be nothing like one."

The Dwarf frowned. "Why were you trying to shoot her?" She looked up the game trail, but there was nothing to see.

"Her?" Now it was Donder's turn to frown. "I just saw fur, but couldn't get a clear shot. I was hoping it was a deer. If I eat another rabbit, I'll shoot myself. Do you know this creature?"

The little Dwarf smiled as she loosened the draw strings on a pouch she had slung over her right shoulder. "I've got flat bread, jerked deer, dried plums, and a few nuts."

"Anything." Donder loosened the string on his bow and returned it to its sheath. "My name is Donder Franks. My friends call me Don. Seeing her hold out the bag, he took two of everything he could readily see. "Thank you very much. What's your name?"

The Dwarf's smile widened. "Entwhistle Bumpas," she answered, watching him munch on the jerky. "I live at Leachenwood, or what's left of it. You're a little short for a man, where were you born?" She glanced up the trail again.

Donder's smile was cut by half. "Leachenwood," he answered with barely a glance.

Entwhistle paused, gripping the drawstrings of her food pouch. "Can't be," she finally got out. I know everyone there and have no memory of you at all."

"Probably wouldn't." He devoured his first piece of flat bread. "I was taken from there when I was five or so, just after my mother died. That was probably before you were born."

"Your father was from the villages of men, wasn't he?"

Donder nodded. "We lived between White Castle and Lake Horn—closer to the lake really.

"The castle is but a shell now." She held the bag out again.

Donder nodded, taking jerky and bread as he did.

"Who was your mother?" Entwhistle asked.

"Rose Elfwyck, daughter of Perryman."

Entwhistle laughed silently, watching him devour the last pieces of bread and jerky while staring at the food pouch. "You must have been pretty hungry to risk shooting the only timber wolf in England."

"Wolf?" The halfling stopped, mid-bite, with a mouthful of jerky. "Never seen one before now. You've got quite a lot of jerky."

"Seleene, the witch called her, was a gift from one of her traders."

"But the witch was killed, yet the wolf lives? How does that work?"

"Very good, I think. Seleene is no longer burdened with the spirit of Ibenus. But, all in all, it has left her very shy of men, or Dwarves for that matter. It took me two years to find her and almost another year to get close."

Donder squinted. You're trying to tame her?"

Entwhistle smiled, nodding. "I have a bet that I can and I believe I am able."

Donder slowly shook his head. "Why would you make such a bet and with whom?"

"To prove a point—girls can do a thing most males can't. The bet is with my father, Billy Bo Bumpus."

"I see."

Donder noted Entwhistle had looked past him and up the

game trail once more. Finally seeing a smile to go with the distraction, he slowly turned to see for himself. There, about forty yards up the trail, stood what she called a wolf. Acting much like a curious dog, the creature watched them both closely.

"See?" she said proudly. "A wild beast wouldn't do such a thing. Ibenus made her unafraid of humans while she lived, but her spirit almost destroyed that after she died. How brave are you?" She reached into the food bag and pulled out a particularly large piece of jerky. Handing it to the halfling, she added, "Step out onto the trail, face her, and then take a bite of it."

"Do what?" Donder's eyes grew big as he glanced at the wolf again.

"You heard me." She gently pushed him out onto the trail. Donder turned, eying the biggest dog he had ever seen.

"Take a bite," Entwhistle encouraged.

Donder obeyed, chewing the tangy morsel as he watched the wolf. Seleene took a half-step forward and then stopped, licking her mouth.

"You've got her attention," the Dwarf whispered. "Now, take two, slow steps forward and hold it out for her."

"What?" Donder's voice weak.

"You heard me. She won't bite you. She knows what you have, and she likes it too."

The halfling rolled his eyes, his gaze ending up on Entwhistle. "She won't bite?"

"Don't think so."

"You're guessing?" Donder squinted at the wolf.

Seleene licked her chops again, but then grunted and turned to trot up the trail and away from Donder.

"Stay there," Entwhistle said encouragingly.

But the hopes of the little Dwarf were diminished as the huge timber wolf, amid glances back at Donder, trotted on and out of sight.

~ * ~

About noon that Monday, Entwhistle's mother, Merrymint, gazed out of the open window in the kitchen and across the field toward Whitestone Road. One of several Dwarf families who chose to live above the ground near Leachenwood, the beautiful, three-foot and eleven-inch redhead quickly came to enjoy the scent of the woods on a beautiful April day. The light scent of rain mixed with fresh-cut hay played with her senses. Her gaze gradually found its way to the barn where her husband, Billy Bo Bumpus, managed the horses and other animals for the Dwarves living below in the caverns of Leachenwood. But the barn was not what had her attention now. Something unusual was in the air—something alarming, something every dwarf feared. She quickly left the kitchen, went out the back door, and then paused at the steps of the back porch. The smell of burning wood was much stronger there. But try as she did, she couldn't see smoke anywhere near or above the trees in the woods. Merrymint slowly stepped from the porch, into the yard, and then looked toward the great, yawning opening of the caves of Leachenwood. The guards were there but Bo wasn't. Looking to her right, she noticed Bo's one-horse cart in the shade of the wild pecan not twenty paces from the front of the barn.

"Time to get someone's attention," she grumbled.

Brushing her red hair from her face, she snatched a three-foot oak pole from where it was hanging next to the back door and struck the hollow, pipe bell hanging close to it. The bell-like sound echoed from the yard and faded into the wood. That action called the guards into plain view, but still no Bo near the Barn. Again and again she struck the pipe until she spotted Bo running from the Barn.

"What is it?" he shouted, stopping under the old pecan.

"Can't ya smell it?" Merrymint pointed toward the woods to the east. "Smoke's on the wind, Bo. If it's a big one, it'll be here soon and the draft of Leachenwood will pull it right down to the last family."

"And we'll be at risk also." Bo knelt, ripped a handful of grass from the ground and tossed it into the air.

Merrymint watched as the grass drifted across the yard and straight toward the caves of Leachenwood. "Smoke from the east!" she yelled at the guards who immediately wheeled and ran back into the cave.

Dullbriar, a thin, blue-eyed dwarf ran up with Borack right behind him. Borack, red-headed brother of Broderick, stood there with his wet blanket and shovel, staring toward the east. Clearly in his sixties, his long, gray hair was pulled back tightly, forming a ponytail low on the back of his head.

"Fairweather's cabin's not far up Whitestone Road," Bo said as he ran up to join Dullbriar and the others. He looked toward the paved road. "He's almost deaf."

"Well," Dullbriar said, "I hope that big nose of his catches the scent."

"Bo!" Merrymint shouted from the porch. "Remember, Trudy is crippled. Go now and check on them! Be quick!"

"Come." Bo nodded toward the two-wheel cart. "Let's go 'n check on my brother."

Now, with Bo and Borack in the wagon seat, Dullbriar knelt in the short bed and held to the back of their seat. Bo reined the Shelties away from the barn and onto Whitestone Road. Dullbriar, trying to protect his knees from the bouncing short bed, frantically searched the woods. Only looking in his forties, he was three times that and then some. Living apart from the 'real' world was not easy and Old Alvis' spell was weakening—now only protecting the woods closely about the great stone of Leachenwood from man's version of normality. Then, as the Whitestone Road paralleled the woods, Borack got a glimpse of someone running toward the barn Bo managed.

"Whoa!" Borack exclaimed as he grabbed the rains from Bo.

"What tha—" Bo started, but he quickly noticed what Borack was pointing at.

Dullbriar jumped from the still-moving cart, waving his hands and yelling at the Dwarf.

"He'll never hear you!" Bo yelled as he quickly jumped from the wagon.

"Go to the house!" Fairweather shouted. "Somethin's happened to Trudy!"

Scrambling back in the cart, the three dwarves raced toward the cabin. As they drew near, smoke could easily be seen rising from the rear of the log and mud structure.

"On the front porch!" Fairweather shouted, still trotting toward them from the woods. "I can't wake her!"

Only then did Bo see his sister-in-law sitting in one of the porch chairs. She looked to be asleep. Strange, black smoke rose from the chimney, adding to the scent of burning wood in the air. Dullbriar and Bo jumped from the cart almost before Borack had time to stop it.

"Check the house," Borack said, sending Dullbriar racing past

Trudy and into the little cabin.

"Bring some water and a wet towel," Dullbriar ordered, patting Trudy's left hand and shoulder. "Her pulse is strong," he added as he gently lifted her left eyelid. "Got a torch?" he asked, glancing at Bo.

Bo spun around and opened the little tack box under the seat. "Got it!" he said as he pulled out a twelve-inch, chrome flashlight.

Running the short distance to the porch, he quickly handed it to Borack.

Flashing it into her eye, Borack quickly shook his head. "The pupils aren't movin'"

"Not movin'?" Fairweather stared at Borack.

"Now don't you get all nervous," Borack said, looking at Fairweather. "I'm gon'na prick her finger."

Fairweather's eyes grew big as the younger dwarf pulled a small dagger from his belt. "Turn her left hand over," he said to Fairweather.

"Don't hurt her badly. Please." Fairweather held to his wife's up-turned hand.

"I don't expect her to feel a thing," Borack said as he gently pricked her finger.

She didn't move at all.

"Looks familiar, don't it?" Bo asked, squinting at Borack.

"You're killin' me here!" Fairweather yelled, his hands cupped behind both ears. "Speak up so's I can hear you! What do you mean?"

Borack looked to Bo.

"You tell 'em," Bo said. "I'm not sayin' it."

Borack, with a deep breath, slowly looked at Fairweather.

"You remember what almost killed Long Barr at the Tree of Sorrows?" he asked loudly.

Fairweather frowned. "Some kind o' spell weren't it?"

Borack nodded. "Do you remember what one o' the Dryads called it?"

Fairweather's eyes grew big as his gaze lowered to the rough boards of the front porch. "Witchen Slumber." He looked back up at Bo. "Can't be. It just can't be. Nobody can do that around here except…"

"Pareen," Borack said. His voice weak.

Bo slowly shook his head. "She's a green witch. Only a white or a black can do such spells."

"But Ethrel Ibenus was vanquished in the field near the Tree of Sorrows. I saw it myself," Dullbriar argued.

"As did we all," Bo agreed. "Truly, she was driven from the wolf by Pareen and the Dryads." He slowly looked to Borack. "Her shadow melted into the grass by the wolf. Surely the Black Witch is dead."

Borack nodded as did the rest.

"Bosh and bunk!" Bo said. "Enough talk. We need to get Trudy to Pareen. I'll get the four-wheeled wagon and we'll be there in less than an hour. Her place's just on the far side of Whitestone Road."

~ * ~

Thirty minutes later, with Borack in the spring seat beside him, Bo reined the Shelties south on Windamere Road toward Grassy Lake crossing. Fairweather sat flat in the wagon's bed, his back against the spring seat with Trudy's back and shoulders in his lap. Dullbriar sat next to him. Feeling every rock in the road, he constantly looked back, checking for Whitestone Road.

"We're not far from the main road," Borack assured them. "Three miles on its paved road and we'll leave it to head west at the Coon Creek trail." He snapped the reins, encouraging the little horses on.

"Good," Fairweather grumbled. "A good, soft dirt trail is better than that black, rock-hard road any day. I'll have blisters on my bruises by the time we get to Coon Creek."

"Should we slow?" Bo looked back at his brother with a slight smile.

"Keep goin' ya field fae," Fairweather said. "Trudy's still not respondin'."

In less than twenty minutes, Bo slowed the wagon and pulled from the paved surface of Whitestone onto a much lesser road that bordered the north side of Coon Creek. Without a word, he stopped the wagon, grabbed a small bucket, and then trotted the short distance to the creek. Scrambling for the reins, Borack turned and watched him scoop the cool water from the fifteen-foot-wide creek.

Fairweather slowly turned and looked up the trail. Looking at Bo watering the horses, he said, "Last time we were here, Long Barr was alive and with us."

Bo frowned, barely affording his older brother a glance. "Glad Pareen didn't hear that. To her, he's still alive."

"Why would you take up for her?" Fairweather asked. "You hardly visit the place anymore."

Bo stood there, with his eyes frozen on the pail of water. "Long was my friend—my best friend. That place around the Tree of Sorrows is too sad for me. His presence is strong there and I can't get him out of my mind when I'm near it."

Dullbriar frowned. "In her house, in the Barn, or in the wood?"

Bo shrugged. "The wood around that place mainly."

Fairweather rested his right arm on the back of the spring seat and looked toward Bo. "When did this start?"

Bo shrugged. "Can't really say." He pushed his moleskin cap to the back of his head, scratching through his hair. "Just over a year ago and only in the forest. My mind seems to spin off some o' his words of wisdom almost like he was sayin' 'em himself." He quickly climbed back into the wagon and tossed the bucket past Fairweather and into the bed. Reining the Shelties on, he added. "Almost two months ago, March I think, somethin' strange happened—somethin' I can't really explain myself."

"Well try for us," Borack prompted.

"Very well. Do you remember that huge old dead oak behind the barn?"

"Yep," Fairweather said, "the one at the edge of the wood and the little creek."

Bo nodded. "It was windy that day and I was comin' out of the forest right there when somethin' slapped me, the limb of a live tree, I think. Anyways, it stopped me stone cold. When it stung my face, it seemed to shout 'Wait!'."

"And…" Dullbriar prompted.

Bo glanced back at the young Dwarf. "Before I could start again, that old tree fell straight across the path where it crosses the creek."

"Coincidence," Borack said, smiling back at Fairweather and Dullbriar.

"Thought that myself," Bo responded. "But the wind was easterly and on my left. The old oak fell with the wind."

"So…" Fairweather said.

"I'll tell you what so," Bo grumbled. "The blow that took my hat off hit me on the right side of my head and it was a green branch that was a good two feet above me."

"Enough of this," Borack said. "We need to get Trudy to Pareen. Encourage the Shelties on. The days of magic, dark or light, are over."

"Shades of Ibenus," Fairweather grumbled as Bo snapped the reins. "Old Alvis's spell only exists an hour in any direction from the Great Stone of Leachenwood. Witchen Slumber? Why would you think of somethin' the last of the Dryads have said anyways?"

Bo glanced back at his brother. "Dryads don't lie. I'm told Pareen visited Dragon's Oak shortly after Long's passing. Do you think—"

"No, I don't think!" Fairweather interrupted. "There's not a soul there. They all left shortly after the last Alvis died. There's only a few halflings that now live some where's close by.

Both Bo and Borack ducked as a large bird flew over them.

"What the devil was that?" Borack asked.

"Horned owl, and a big one," Fairweather said. "It disappeared into an ash not twenty yards ahead of us."

"What of the Int?" Dullbriar asked as he searched the ash. "His name is Limbisconn. He's the last Druid we know of. If he still lives, then so does Long Barr. If that is so, then Trudy may still have a chance."

~ * ~

It was only a few minutes after Dullbriar's comment when Bo reined the Shelties away from the creek and onto another wagon path. The path itself was much like the coon creek trail, but it was also much different in some respects. Red and white clover seemed to be almost everywhere, virtually refusing the Johnson grass and hogweed a place. Its patches were only broken by the cattails bordering the much smaller creek on their right. At the edges of the wood, wild plums and buttercups grew everywhere.

Fairweather nudged Bo. "Look different to you?"

Bo nodded. "Last time I was here, the weeds were higher than my head."

"Aware of that," Borack added, seemingly distracted by something. "Me and six of your archers worked almost every day for three months on this place. You won't recognize the old cabin; cause the greater part of it's been tore down and rebuilt. There's a cold water well right inside the kitchen as well as one outside near the little barn they built."

"I see," Bo said. "Did Pareen help with the flowers and stuff?"

Borack shrugged, glancing up at the trees as they passed under them. "Don't know much about Green Witches and even less about Wizards. But at night, and during the days we worked on the house and Barn, you could hear things movin' about in the woods and the fields."

"Dry leaves rustled where there weren't none," Fairweather said with a chuckle. He looked to Borack. "What's got your goat? You keep checkin' the trees like somethin's in 'em."

"Big owl." Borack's voice was low.

"Hawk most likely," Dullbriar suggested. "No owl flies in the daylight."

Bo glanced back at his brother. The smile on his brother's face echoed the hope he was keeping alive for his wife.

Dullbriar looked to Fairweather also. "You're talkin' about Dryads again aren't you?"

"Yep," the old dwarf replied. "Borack was right. 'Twas an owl —a Great Horned to be exact. When you see owls fly in the daylight, you can bet it's bein' guided by another."

"Then the Dryads are somewhere close," Bo said. "What about Long?" Snapping the reins again, he took a new interest in the trees as did the others.

Although Bo's last question was low, Borack caught it and just slowly shook his head. As they approached a fence made of field and river stone, Bo slowed the Shelties to a stop. He stood in the wagon and peered over the six-foot structure at a roof made of split cedar shingles. Looking through the opening in the fence he could see the Tree of Sorrows in the distance to his right. Dozens of Dragon flies played over the field—some blue, some bright green, and others yellow and red.

"Don't remember this," Bo whispered.

"Tree of Sorrows," Fairweather said. "Long Bow named it when the witch Ibenus trapped Pareen in the tree.

"I know that," Bo grumbled. "I meant the cabin's different as well as the grounds."

"That's Dolby Bramble," Dullbriar said, quickly rising to his knees looking toward the house.

Long grey hair and an equally long beard, the old Bowman sat on the front porch squinting through his bushy eyebrows at those in the wagon. He barely afforded them a nod.

"He's got a bow," Bo said. "Is he still an archer."

Fairweather smiled. "Yep and can cut an apple stem at forty paces." Fairweather looked toward Dolby. "Is she here?" he asked loudly.

Dolby nodded, pointing with his thumb toward the cabin.

Bo slowly reined the Shelties toward the front porch. "Don't look the same at all—new porch, roof, siding, windows, and even a stone chimney. And there's a big lean-to on the far side."

Bo slowed the wagon just paces from the porch and looked back toward the Tree of Sorrows.

"He's not there, Bo," another voice said from the porch.

Quickly turning, Bo looked into the smiling face of a young, blonde-haired, girl of nineteen or so. Her bright, blue eyes echoed the smile. She was still wearing the silent, silver whistle on a silver chain around her neck. She was also holding the Stick of Eefron. Quickly stopping the horses, Bo handed the reins to Borack, removed his hat, and stood with all except Fairweather, who was still holding Trudy.

Part 2
Expellax – Killing of the Spell

"Pareen Willingham, my Lady of the Wood." Bo's voice was soft. He bowed as did the others. "We have a problem. "One of ours is stricken and we are not sure of the affliction."

He looked back at Trudy.

As Pereen stepped from the porch, still looking at Bo, her smile diminished somewhat. "It is good to see you, Billy Bo Bumpus. I am sorry you are angry with me. I had little choice in the happenings that freed me from the tree or put Long Barr in my place. Have you been well?"

"I am, My Lady, and I don't hold you responsible for Long's demise or any other thing. It's just that…" Bo looked down at the Shelties and ran his fingers through his long, red hair. "We were close, very close. Every time I chose to get near this area, his memory comes rushing back to me making it very hard to continue." He looked back to Fairweather and Trudy. "My brother's wife seems asleep and we cannot wake her. I fear she's been spelled."

"Spelled?" Pareen eased closer to the wagon bed. "Fairweather?"

"My apologies, My Lady," the old Dwarf said. "I cannot stand."

Pareen's smile widened. She looked to Dullbriar. "Please help Fairweather bring Trudy inside and I'll have a look."

As Bo jumped from the wagon, he was distracted by the shadow of a large bird. It flew across the yard, disappearing in the oaks to his right. Turning, he could see Fairweather and Dullbriar had Trudy upon the porch but were hesitating at the open door.

"Well, go on in," Borack prompted.

Struggling to get a better hold on Trudy, Fairweather nodded toward a trim, dark-haired man standing in the family room. His black mustache, long and full, disappeared in his chest-length beard. Dressed as a woodsman, leather pants and deerskin shirt, he stood staring at those at the doorway.

"John Schmidt," Pareen said. "He's a friend. He can be trusted. Go on in."

Bo, seeing his brother's feet still frozen to the porch, eased up to the door opening and peeped inside at the man. "Seven feet or better," Bo whispered. "His head's barely six inches from the ceiling. Bo, squinting at the big man, couldn't see a smile. His mustache was so thick his mouth was all but hidden.

"John, my friends call me," he said, toasting them with his cup. "Got fresh coffee for those who will have it," he added.

"Go on," Bo said again with a gentle nudge to the small of Fairweather's back. "He's smilin' at ya."

"Smilin'? Can't see his mouth." Fairweather, with a keen eye on the tall man, eased inside with Bo and Borack right behind him. Dullbriar, however, opted to tend to the Shelties.

"It's his big, blue eyes," Borack said with a laugh, "and his cheeks are up."

"In here," the man said. His tone remarkably friendly, he gestured toward the lean-to doorway.

"Go on, Fairweather," a now laughing Pareen said. "He won't bite you."

"A man friend in your cabin, Pareen?" Borack said as he walked toward the lean-to doorway.

Although she couldn't readily see in, Pareen knew there was a smile under that red beard.

"Am I not allowed friends, Master Dwarf?" Pareen followed them toward the room. "Go on," she prompted, seeing Fairweather was still nervous about passing so close to the strange man. "He's a friend and is just searching for his daughter. Someone has taken her he believes."

"I see." Fairweather stepped past the big man and into the lean-to bedroom."

Bo stopped, watching Pareen follow his brother into the room. Looking up at John, he asked, "What's she look like, Mr. Schmidt?"

"It's John to my friends. Her name is Trudy. She's blonde, blue-eyed, about five feet, five inches tall, and doesn't like dark places, especially the woods at night. And she—"

"Put her by the fireplace and stoke it nice and hot," Pareen interrupted as she walked briskly from the bedroom.

Wheeling to her right and around the big woodsman, she hurried straight toward the cupboard, left of the stove in the corner.

Taking a long-spouted teapot from one of its shelves, she quickly turned to Borack. "Well water, half full, and put it to boil in the fireplace. Quickly now."

"Fire?" Bo eyed the fireplace, its bed of coals was barely glowing, but the cabin was remarkably warm. His brother was making a pallet of quilts very close to it. "It's mid-April and not that cold and—"

"Now, Bo!" Pareen ordered. "I don't have time to explain. Trudy's in a bind and it's tightening by the minute."

"Yes Ma'am." Bo hurried to the tender box and began stoking the fireplace as Borack tended the teapot at the pump in the kitchen.

Sticking to his place by the stove, John watched the goings-on. Pareen was at Trudy's right side with a black, leather bag. Rummaging through it, she pulled out a small, flexible, and clear tube about eighteen inches long.

"Where'd that come from?" Borack asked as he peeped in from the kitchen, holding the teapot. "You're startin' ta act like Bright Helen's grandfather."

"Heat that up and be quick about it, Borack," Pareen ordered.

"Yes, My Lady," the Dwarf said, quickly making his way to the fireplace. In little time, he had the pot boiling. He looked to Pereen. White ash stained the bottom of his red beard. "Still dizzy from blowin' on them embers, but the water's nice 'n hot right now I think."

Pareen glanced up at Bo. "Get a metal pan from the kitchen. We need more hot water." She turned back to Trudy and started looking at her fingernails."

"What's those?" Fairweather nodded toward the little bottle Pareen had sat on the hearth. It contained what looked to be several, pea-sized, blue-green marbles.

"Gifts from Dragon's Oak," Pareen explained.

Fairweather looked at Bo as he set the metal pan of water on the wire grate over the coals. "At a loss here, brother," Fairweather said, his voice low. "Don't know what she's doin' and little of what she's talkin' about."

Borack sat down on the hearth, looking at them both. "Dragon Oak's long gone—nothin' but a memory now. Those left here are more like our Bright Helen, I think. She's the Professor's grandchild, but she can hear the Int."

"But the Elves are gone," Dullbriar added from the bedroom doorway. "Most now-a-days don't even know what an Elf is. The time of man is with us today."

Pareen glanced back at the three. "I wouldn't say that. Diluted by time perhaps, but still here none-the-less. There is one who lives not far from here and near Lake Horn. He is quite comfortable there and doesn't need the 'Promise of Alvis' to hide behind."

"Dragon's Oak now refers to that place," John added.

Dullbriar frowned. "But the old spell protects our home at Leachenwood. We—"

"Wait a minute," Fairweather interrupted, staring at Pareen. "You went there?"

Pareen smiled as she sat down on the floor next to Trudy. "Two years ago I visited a lady named Francis Andoria. She looked to be in the end of her years, but still very bright in our ways." Pareen nodded toward the little bottle. "If I had them, perhaps Long would still be with us."

"Then..." Fairweather paused, looking at the little pill bottle. "Ya know what's wrong with her don't ya?"

"I believe so," Pareen answered. Through a slight smile, she added, "But we'll soon see. Is the water in the teapot hot?"

Borack quickly checked the teapot. "Yes, My Lady, it is."

Pareen quickly straightened out the flexible tube, took out one of the little pills, and then looked to Fairweather. "You two have a lot of years left. Now, hold her mouth open. Bo, hold her legs down and Borack, get by her head and hold her arms still." She looked to Dullbriar. "When the dark curse rises from her mouth, pour the water from the teapot into the pan and hand me the pot as quickly as you can."

Dullbriar knelt by the pot and watched Fairweather open Trudy's mouth. Pareen then gingerly slipped the little tube into Trudy's mouth and eased it down her throat. Slipping one of the little pills into the tube, Pareen blew the little, blue-green marble into Trudy's stomach and quickly pulled out the tube. She then tossed Dullbriar a small pair of gloves and put on a pair herself.

Fairweather looked to Pareen. "What kind 'o pill is that?"

"It is no pill," Pareen said, her voice soft. "She is not sick but under a terrible spell."

"Witchen Slumber," Bo said.

Pareen nodded. "It'll take a little bit for the spell to sense the stone. We must be ready," she added, glancing at Dullbriar.

"Bless my beard," Fairweather managed to say as tears welled up in his eyes. "And the green marble you slipped down the tube is…"

Now, all eyes were on Pareen.

"It's an amethyst, my little friends." Pareen's voice was soft. "Two years ago, under Francis' instruction, I visited the eastern shore of Lake Horn. There, within the great stone bluffs, is a place called Phagan's Rift."

"The Eastern Elves…" Bo sat back on his haunches, looking at Pareen. "I thought it to be only a fable. Does old Phagan still live? He would be last of the wizards I believe."

Pareen smiled, watching Trudy closely. "He still lives, but—"

Pareen's voice trailed off as she noticed the strange looking, black smoke begin to rise from Trudy's mouth.

"It comes," Fairweather said, now trying to move his head away from the shadowy substance.

"Quickly now, Dullbriar," Pareen said.

"Bless my axe!" Bo exclaimed as he shoved the metal pan closer to Dullbriar.

"I got it!" Dullbriar immediately poured the boiling water into the pan and handed the empty teapot to Pareen.

Black as soot, and the size of a good apple, the spell slowly twisted around and around as it hovered only inches over Trudy's still open mouth.

John's eyes grew big. Slowly stepping inside the doorway, he watched what was happening.

Holding the teapot's lid tightly closed with her gloved, left hand, Pareen blocked the spout opening with the index finger of her right. Easing the spout as close to the spell as she dared, the Green Witch removed her finger and seemingly poked the rotating black apparition with the end of the spout. The hot void within the pot drew the spell inside. A wet sounding splutter-thump announced the capture of the spell as it was sucked into the, all but glowing, teapot.

"Out of my way!" Pareen ordered as she scrambled around Trudy for the fireplace.

Dodging the hot teapot in Pareen's hands, the Dwarves quickly moved away from the hearth.

John moved closer as he watched Pareen shove the spout of the pot deep into the glowing ashes of the fireplace then jerk her hands from it. "Sounds like bacon frying in a pan," he said.

Fairweather nodded. "The spell's dyin'."

"Shhh," Pareen hissed. "Listen, and bring the water pan close to the fire."

Bo quickly sat the water pan upon the hearth between Pareen and Borack. "I believe it's stopped hissin'," he said, glancing at Pareen.

"Hand me the poker." Pareen nodded to the stand directly behind Borack.

Borack quickly turned and grabbed the poker.

"That's good," Pareen said. "Now, pick up the teapot and set it in the water. It, as well as the remnants of the spell need to cool off quickly, but not so as to crack the crystals."

The Dwarf leader of the archers gingerly slipped the curved end of the poker through the teapot handle, lifted it from the ashes, and then set it hissing and bubbling into the water of the pan.

Scrambling from the hearth, Both Borack and Bo set down next to Fairweather and Dullbriar to watch what came next. All eyes were now on the teapot.

"Ohhh boys…" Pareen's melodious tone, quickly garnered their attention. But, she said not another word, only nodded toward Trudy, still lying on the carpet behind her.

Fairweather's eyes grew big. "Great Benjamin's Dragon!" he exclaimed, jumping to his feet. "Her eyes are open an' lookin' right at me!"

"Bless my disbelief," Bo said as he slowly stood with the others to watch Fairweather take Trudy into his arms.

With her eyes batting wildly, Trudy looked all about the little room. "Where am I?" she finally managed.

"Alive, My Lady. Alive." Tears streamed down Fairweather's face disappearing into his beard.

Bo eased up, smiling down at her. "Welcome back. You're at Pareen's home near the Tree of Sorrows."

She looked at her husband. "Why are you crying? I hardly ever see you cry."

"Well…" Fairweather paused to wipe his eyes with his shirt sleeve. "Maybe it's about time."

"What do you last remember?" Pareen asked.

"I was in my own home, rocking in my own chair before the fireplace, and listening to Fair chop up some turnips for our supper. He already had the pork roast in the cooking pot over the fire and the whole cabin smelled wonderful. Then, I heard the strangest thing coming from the fireplace. Before I had a chance to figure that out, the whole thing seemed to explode right there in front of me." She glanced at Fairweather. "I must of fainted 'cause the next thing I knew, I was here."

"Welcome back," John Schmidt said smiling broadly.

"Yes indeed." Fairweather glanced at the big woodsman. "I heard the commotion and ran into the room to find Trudy lying on the floor in the middle of at least a half-dozen little fires. I quickly put them out, scooped her up in my arms, and then sat her down in one of the porch chairs. I was headin' for Bo's house when I spotted the wagon."

Bo stepped closer, looking at Trudy. "What kind o' sound was it that you heard?"

"Laughter—a giggling kind of laughter I believe. That's when the fireplace exploded. Tumbled me backwards and right out of the rocker it did. But, before everything went to black, I looked into the blue eyes of a young girl." She looked at Fairweather. "I don't know who she was or where she came from 'cause I fainted right then."

"Elisa…" John quickly stepped closer, handing his coffee cup to Dullbriar. "Did ya see her face perhaps?"

Trudy, with Fairweather's help, struggled to a sitting position, looking at the big man. "Not very well I'm afraid. I was on my way out, so to speak, when I noticed her. But…I think she had blonde hair."

The big man smoothed back his hair. "At least a small ray of hope is better than none at all," he said softly.

"Tell me sir," Bo said, garnering the big man's attention. "How does a name like Schmidt come with a Scottish accent?"

His smile was back with a bit of a shrug. "My father was German. He left us for the sea one fine day and never came back. My mother's name was McIntosh. She raised me with her father's help." He looked back at Pareen. "Dear Lady, can you tell me what has befallen my Elisa?"

Pareen slowly nodded. "She has fallen prey to a black witch, I fear. Ethrel Ibenus has survived somehow. Perhaps she claimed one of the Dryads for a short time."

"Possessed?" John stared at the Dwarves, but there was no help there. "This Ibenus woman is doin' this to my Elisa?"

"She's a crone, Mr. Schmidt, and a black witch ta boot," Bo explained. "I thought with the Professor's help and his Bright Helen, we had finally done for her."

"Evidently not," Borack said. "You can't just slap the hand of an old crone and expect to walk away without a limp."

"Indeed," Bo added. "We done much more than just slap her hand. We tried to kill her and did for the most part."

John squinted, looking from Bo, to Borack, and then back to Bo again. "How can one 'mostly' kill someone?"

"Her spirit still lives," Pareen said. She looked to Borack. "Hand me the teapot. It should be cool by now."

Borack paused at the metal pan, staring down at the little teapot. "It's dead, right?"

"It will not harm you," Pareen said as she knelt by Trudy. After spreading a white handkerchief out on the rug, she looked back at Borack. "Pour the contents out upon the cloth."

Borack knelt by the handkerchief, opened the top of the teapot, and then tilted it above the white cloth. Out rolled thirteen, egg-shaped, pea-sized stones as black and shiny as onyx.

"Thirteen stones?" Borack asked as Bo stepped closer.

Each stone was not exactly smooth but had many, flat sides and reflected every point of light in the little room.

"Expellax," Pareen said as she quickly gathered them up in the handkerchief. We need to take these to the Professor, and then talk with Bright Helen. To work, these must be ground into a fine, dust-like powder." She looked to Bo. "I trust they are both still there."

Bo nodded. "Entwhistle, my daughter, visited them only last week."

Fairweather leaned close to Bo and whispered, "Your daughter's close to Helen is she?"

Bo nodded. "They're workin' on tamin' the Black Witch's wolf, Seleene. Entwhistle thinks—"

"What?" Borack interrupted. His voice most loud. "That wolf? You'd put that child in harm's way again. Have you two lost ya senses?"

Bo took a half-step forward, putting him and Borack nose to nose. "Borack Cliffspring," he said loudly, "would you abandon Trudy Bumpas? After all, she was afflicted by the Black Witch also. Is she not worth the savin?"

Now, all eyes were on Borack. None but the big woodsman where smiling. Somehow, he found humor where the heat of the moment simply overshadowed it.

"Assumptions, assumptions my little friends!" the giant of a man exclaimed. He pulled his double-bladed axe from its sheath on his belt and stepped toward the little group, grimacing as he did so.

All gave ground but Pareen and Fairweather. Fairweather grabbed his wife, shielding her as best he could. John stopped, looking down at Pareen and very close to Fairweather and Trudy. His smile quickly returned as he slipped his axe back into its sheath.

"There ya go. Do ya see," John said, laughing at the other Dwarves. "Ya all were so scared ya could no find your blades." He nudged Fairweather with the toe of his right boot. "He would o' gave ground to, save for his wife. Love alone kept him there and none else." He looked to Pareen. "That bein' said, why do ya think the young lass stood her ground? She had no weapon."

"Well…" Bo looked to Borack, but remained stumped.

"She knew you," Trudy guessed.

John laughed out loud. "And the prize goes to the lady on the carpet. Love kept Fairweather with you 'cause love and worth was still there. Even though the Black Witch had touched her, he knew she would remain the same person when her spell was driven from her. I've been cutting, huntin, and gatherin for Pareen for over a year now and have come ta know a few of her friends—Entwhistle and Helen bein' two of 'em. The one they are seekin' now is the only wolf in all of England. They both see her worth. She has no evil aura, Entwhistle told me." He smiled, glancing at Pareen. "I don't know much about this 'aura' thing, but they both see worth in the animal since the witch no longer has sway over it."

"Then…" Fairweather slowly looked to Pareen. "From what I've just seen, Ibenus not only lives, but is now walking among us."

"With my daughter," the woodsman added, now looking at Pareen also.

The Green Witch slowly shook her head. "Tomorrow I must travel to the Professor's home and see Bright Helen. I would feel much better about it if I had company between here and there."

"I'll go," volunteered the woodsman. With raised eyebrows, he smiled at the Dwarves as though daring them to venture out also.

"So will we all," Fairweather said. "I'll post guards both here and at our home and put an amethyst in every window if I must. We must continue this quest until we are certain the Black Witch no longer lives."

"Good." Pareen, smiled at the woodsman. "Then, we will leave for Coon Creek trail to the Hollow Oak early tomorrow. You are welcome to stay the night here if you choose.

"That we will," Bo said. "But…" Bo looked at Pareen with a squint. "Once one steps into the Hollow Oak, we can't just think on the shift-a-robe in Bright Helen's room. Walkin' out o' that uninvited would be a bit awkward wouldn't ya think?"

Pareen slowly nodded. "Then, we'll set our mind on the Great Ash in the lower part of the Professor's back grounds."

"Good," Borack agreed. "Don't much like the houses of men anyways—too many odors make me dizzy."

"You've lost me again," John said. "The Creek Trail leads to Whitestone Road. What does this Hollow Oak Road thing have ta do with anything? Don't think I know where that one is."

Fairweather chuckled silently. "It's not a road, my big friend— at least not one you can walk on. To you, it will be a lesson in trust I believe. Pareen has just pulled you deeper into a world most men will never see." He slowly stood from his wife's side, squinting up at the big man. "There must be more ta you than meets the eye, John Schmidt. For a Green Witch to trust a man, he must be truly different."

Part 3
To Hunt a Witch

The next morning began dark and dank. Storms had moved in over the night, leaving heavy, gray clouds, wet ground, and a chill that made mid-April seem like February again. Fairweather, Bo, Borack, and Dullbriar waited on the front porch, continuously taunted by the aroma of the fresh biscuits and fried ham Pareen and Trudy were cooking in the kitchen.

"Anybody hungry?" Borack asked.

All nodded but Dullbriar.

Borack's eyes narrowed as he looked at Dullbriar. "You ate already?"

"Kind of," the young Dwarf answered.

"What does 'kind of' mean?" Bo asked.

"Oreos," Dullbriar said.

"Good grief," Fairweather said with a chuckle. "The world of men is truly rubbing off on this one."

Just then, the screen door opened. John ducked under the frame and stepped onto the porch, looking at the Dwarves. "Somethin' before the trip?" He handed Bo a small basket covered with a white cloth. "Will ya be takin' milk or water? We have no coffee."

Borack quickly drew close to Bo, eying the covered basket. "I smell ham."

"And biscuits," Bo added. He slowly uncovered the basket to reveal at least a dozen biscuit sandwiches.

"Water'll be fine for us," Borack said, taking the first, fist-sized sandwich.

"Eat quick," John prompted. "We leave just as soon as the Fair Lady gets dressed. She wants to be at the Oak before nine." He turned to Bo. "For the like of me, it's after seven and she said the Professor's house is a good ways off."

Fairweather chuckled. "You sleep in the house at night?"

"In the lean-to." John frowned slightly. "What did ya expect? Ya all slept in the living room before the fireplace did ya not?"

"Just looking out for Pareen," Fairweather added.

"And that we all should. I'm Pareen's cousin."

"Fairweather slowly looked to Bo. "She has a…""

"Cousin's the word you're lookin' for," John said with a grumble. "Friend's the one you should find. Now tend to those biscuits and I'll bring some glasses and a pitcher of water."

"Where are you from?" Bo asked as John started back inside.

Pausing, the big man looked to Bo. "East of Lake Horn," he answered and then shut the screen door behind him.

"Bless my beard," Fairweather said. His voice only a whisper. "He's one of 'em."

"One of what," Borack sputtered with a mouth full of biscuit and ham.

"Phagan's Rift and the Eastern Elves, you ogre." Fairweather said. "Didn't ya not hear 'em. He's one o' those halflings from Dragon's Haunt—the forest right above old Phagan's place."

Borack, almost choking on his biscuit, stared at Bo. "That place's been gone seven hundred years or more as well as the White Elves. "They don't even call it Dragon's Haunt anymore. It's all owned by some Scotsman and well outside of Old Alvis' spell. They all live and work in the world of men."

"Pareen eased the screen door open, stepped out onto the front porch in front of John and then looked at the Dwarves. "Don't lament the past. It will sway how you act in the present."

Bo stopped mid-bite, looking up at the big man. "The Fae folk are still in the forest north of the Rift?"

"Not everywhere," John admitted. "Just where the old…" John's words seemed to lose their strength as he glanced at Pareen.

Fairweather squinted. "Old what? I heard that. Old what?"

"Never mind," Pareen said. "John and Borack have our horses fed and ready. Let us leave now for the Hollow Oak."

Still grumbling about John's 'old' comment, the Dwarves turned to Pareen.

"Good enough," Fairweather said as the Dwarves headed for their wagon.

Taking the lead, Pereen and John headed down the trail toward Coon Creek Road on horseback. The Dwarves stuck to the wagon. In twenty-five minutes they were in sight of the Whitestone Road. Pereen slowed, looking back at the others. No sooner had she done that, than something shot between him and Borack, grabbed Bo's moleskin cap, and then took to the trees with it.

"What the blazes was that!" Bo exclaimed. His attempt to save his hat left him with two hands full of his own hair.

"An owl," Fairweather said. "I saw it clear. Went into this big oak right above us and just vanished."

"Vanished?" Bo squinted up in the limbs and leaves above him. "The blazin' buzzard's got my hat!"

"Lead them across, Pereen," Bo grumbled from the wagon.

"Across?" John stood in the saddle, looking at the wide, paved highway. "We're not takin' the highway?"

"We're at the tree," Bo said, smiling at the woodsman. He pointed toward a huge, white oak on the far side of the highway. Towering above the rest, it looked to be thirty yards from the road and well over a hundred feet tall.

"It's missin' its middle," John said. "It should be dead."

Laughing, Fairweather replied, "Let us go. We'll cross and I'll string a rope on the far side of the tree to tie the horses to. They'll be hid well enough from the road there."

Once there, everyone dismounted save the woodsman. He sat astride his horse, firmly planted in the saddle, and gazed at the huge, five-foot by three-foot hole in the trunk of the tree.

"Get off your horse you halfling," Fairweather said as the Dwarves laughed. "How long has it been since you used the Elfin part of your brain? It's time you stopped believin' the things you see and seein' the things you believe in."

"What?" John stared at the Dwarf and then looked to Pareen. "Do ya know, My Lady, what the wee one is talkin' about?"

Pareen's smile widened. "John, this is something you'll have to see and do with us. Just follow Bo."

John dismounted, tied his horse to Fairweather's rope, and then walked toward Bo. "Well, let us go if we're goin'."

"Very well." Bo stepped toward the big tree, ducked, and then went into the shadows of its yawning hole.

John's chin slowly dropped. Stooping down, he gazed into the darkness. "I'll no believe my eyes," he whispered, easing closer.

Fairweather, standing right behind John with Borack, winked and nodded toward John still stooping over. "Just stick your head in a little and you can see 'em."

"See 'em?" John eased his head and shoulders into the cavity.

"Now!" Fairweather said and the two Dwarves shoved the big woodsman as hard as they were able.

"No-no!" The big man, all seven feet of him, went straight into the tree, disappearing also.

~ * ~

Bo, standing at the side of a huge Ash tree at the lower end of the Professor's back yard, watched as John stumbled out on the far side of it with Fairweather and Borack still pushing him. Pereen and the others were right behind them.

"Damn!" John exclaimed, sliding to a halt. He straightened up, looked back at the Dwarves, and then at the huge Ash. "How are we gettin' back, or do I wan'na know?"

Fairweather smiled. "We have to call the Dragon of course."

"What?" John glared down at the Dwarf who instantly burst out laughing as did Pareen and the others.

But that moment of levity was short-lived and ended by the slamming of the Professor's back door. The orange and white Corgi running toward them brought an instant smile to Bo's face. He didn't have to guess who the blonde-haired lady on the back porch was."

"Helen," Bo said softly.

But the Corgi stopped abruptly only half-way there, his attention on something in the woods to his right.

"Zee boy." Fairweather eased his hand to his axe and slowly stepped toward where Zee was looking. "What do you see my little friend?"

"No!" Helen said loudly as she ran toward them.

"There…" Bo whispered as he pointed toward a shadowy figure under a fir tree and all of ten paces from the edge of the back yard.

"A dog?" Dullbriar guessed.

"Yea, that, and a big one ta boot," Borack added.

Fairweather paused, looking at Helen. "Seleene?"

Helen nodded.

Fairweather squinted. "Bright Helen, what do ya see in that creature?"

"Sorrow, I guess," Helen answered. "She is the only one of her kind in all of England and in bad need of a friend. I also see trust and a complete dislike for the Black Witch."

Everyone walked toward Helen Durkin. John trailed the group.

"She cares for the creature," he explained. "When all remained afraid of her because of the Witch Ibenus, only three have come to her aid. That bein' Helen, Bo's daughter Entwhistle, and Pareen."

Bo turned back to John. "You know my daughter?"

John nodded slightly, looking down at the grass between him and the others. "I've been searchin' for my daughter for over a year now. Pareen, Helen, and Entwhistle have been my only helpers thus far. The attack on Fairweather's wife is as close as I have ever been to locating her. When Elisa saw me, she ran from Fair's house with a speed no human could match. I am almost without means ta continue but I cannot find the will to quit. My wife is dead and Elisa is all I have left in the world."

Alerted by Zee's soft woof, everyone could see the silhouetted figure leave the fir tree for the woods beyond.

Helen stroked Zee's head. "Go if you like," she said softly.

"You don't need a thing but the resolve to continue," Bo said to John. We have your back if needs be. We have a stake in this as well."

"Lift up your head," Fairweather said loudly. "You go 'round feelin' sorry for yourself an' that Black Witch'll have your head and perhaps one of ours also. Now, how'd you know your daughter was in my house?"

Now, all eyes were on the woodsman as he slowly looked at Fairweather. "Seleene...I follow the timber wolf don't ya see? Seems ta me the creature has a fear-hate complex for the Black Witch—one that will live within her until one or the other is destroyed. Elisa left the cabin some time ago for a stroll in the woods to gather things—herbs, nuts, mushrooms, berries and such. When she didn't return, I went out lookin'. Clean around the south side of Lake Horn I tracked her and on west across the Green River to Windamere. Spent almost a month there showin' pictures and talkin' ta those who seen her. Then, at Windamere, I chanced upon a lady who gave her a room for the night. She said my daughter left with a man for the Gray Rock Community."

Borack looked at Pareen. "That's here and Seleene is here as well."

"But Elisa isn't," John added. "I watch the wolf closely. When Elisa is close, the creature's hackles are up." He turned and pointed toward a maple tree under a group of much larger oaks. "Look closely at the base of the maple."

"Bless my beard," Fairweather said. "What's the wolf doin' now?"

"She watches Helen I think," Pareen answered. "Some animals can see things we cannot."

Fairweather slowly turned and looked to Pareen. She was smiling. "You knew all of this didn't you?"

The smile held, but neither nod, nor word came from the Green Witch.

"Sooo…" Fairweather grumbled. "We must fight this evil one again.

Pareen's smile widened. "I hope to support Bright Helen, Master Dwarf. She will be with us. Bo has committed the Dwarves to helping John find his daughter. That being said, I believe we will all meet the Black Witch when that happens." She raised her eyebrows at the old Dwarf. "John, clearly a man, has offered his services. Would you not join in with the others to help us?"

Fairweather noticed Bo was feeling for his hat. "Not there is it?" he asked with a grin. Owl done ate it by now."

"We gon'na help John anyways. You be with Pereen or not?" Bo asked, looking at his brother with a bit of a squint.

At that same instant, even before Bo's brother could form an answer, something dropped from the sky and landed in the grass between Bo and Fairweather.

"My hat!" Bo quickly snatched it from the ground and looked to where Helen was pointing.

"There he is," Borack said. "He's perched on a limb 'bout twenty feet above us. It *is* a Great Horned Owl."

"Look closer," Helen prompted.

"Bless my bow," Borack said weakly. "There's a Dryad on the creature. The way it's dressed, it almost looks like a part of the tree."

True enough, the rare creature looked to be all of twelve inches tall, dark complexion-perhaps a shade of greenish-brown, and frizzed, black hair.

"With you," Fairweather said, his voice strong. "If the Dryads are with our Helen, then the Druid will be in those oaks as well."

"They will," Bo said as he held out his hat. It had an owl's feather in it.

"Good enough," Bo said. "Then together we will once again

face down the Black Witch." He looked to Helen. "What of the Hobuerich? Will they again be with her as well?"

Helen's eyes grew big, looking from Pareen to Bo and then back again.

"I think not," Borack said. "The world of men have done for them."

Now, all eyes were on the Dwarves.

"It is true," Bo admitted. "Two years ago or so, old Alvis' spell, the one that conceals our existence, weakened and withdrew from the Yellow Grass area. It weren't long before an English farmer crossed paths with one of their Hagstroms and—"

"You mean one of those weird horses the Hobs ride?" Helen said.

"The same, My Lady," Bo answered. "The farmer followed the beast to the Yellow Grass and the Hobuerich Caverns where they lived. Undiscovered by the Hobs, the farmer fled the place and then returned with a small army. A huge pile of blackened wood and ashes is all that's left of the caverns."

The Dwarves slowly removed their hats and looked to Helen.

"Bright Helen," Fairweather said, "we live in caverns as well. We've crossed paths with men on occasion but have not fared near as badly. But, they have never seen where we live. If we lose the Alvis spell also, will the same fate befall us all?"

"No Sir!" The woodsman's voice very loud.

Fairweather slowly turned to John. "You are big and powerful, John Schmidt, but those who destroyed the Yellow Grass Caverns were many. Would you stand with us again' such as that?"

John took a deep breath. His face somewhat sad. "Don't judge us too harshly, Master Dwarf. Men, as a whole, usually fear what they don't understand. The Hobuerich were evil beings and were seen for just that. I know several men who know of you and yours. They call you men—men of Leachenwood. Some of your people have helped widows and old people who needed food and such in the winter, and found children lost in the woods." He nodded toward Borack. "Just last year, I am told this one beat the pants off a poacher when he caught him taking advantage of a farmer's young daughter who was collectin' berries and mushrooms in the wood."

"Had nothin' to do with pants," Borack grumbled as the other Dwarves laughed. "They fell off when he tried to get away."

Fairweather cupped his ears with his hands and looked at Borack. "I was told you gave 'em to the girl."

"There was money in his pockets," Borack said with a growl. "Don't you think she should have it?"

"We're getting off the subject at hand," Pareen interrupted. She stepped closer to Helen. "Ibenus holds sway over John's daughter, and no doubt has her eyes set on the demise of those who tried to kill her or anyone who would get in her way." She paused, looking at Helen. "The Oak Druid calls you Bright Helen. He sees a power in you that none else can have except perhaps the Dryads. Again, we are going to ask much of you. Does the wolf truly trust you and can she find John's daughter?"

All the Dwarves slowly pulled their hats off and looked to Helen.

Helen nodded. "I believe she can find Ibenus whether she resides in Elisa or not."

Bo looked at Helen. "Do you think, Limbisconn, the Oak Druid will help us find her?"

Helen hesitated, looking a little confused as well as fearful. "I must say I'm well off my comfort zone here."

Still holding their hats, all the Dwarves looked to Helen.

"Bright Helen," Bo started, all but wadding up his hat. "Does that mean you will not help us?"

"Certainly not. I will help you. It just means the last time we went after the Black Witch it scared the bageebers out of me."

Gradually, the smiles found their way back to the Dwarves as they put their hats back on.

"Dear Helen." Pareen was now smiling also. "Our best is all any of us can do. The feather on Bo's hat was a message—one from the Druid I'm thinking. I believe Limbisconn is watching you right now."

"Then…" Helen looked to Pareen. "I will rely on you for direction. What must we do?"

Pareen smiled. "You must first go and tell your grandparents that you will be with us. Will that be a problem?"

Hellen's smile widened. "Of course it will. Grandmother's gon'na have kittens, again. She's already nervous about Seleene. She's seen her in the woods near our yard several times already."

"Go and talk with them now," Bo said. "If you like, one of us will go with you."

"Bring a change of clothes and perhaps a jacket," Pareen said.

"I've got this," Helen said.

She then turned and trotted toward the back porch. Halfway there, she noticed Martin and Narbie standing at the kitchen window. Her grandmother's finger tips had already found their way to her mouth. Her expression could only be defined as worry. Once through the back door, Helen walked down the short hallway and paused at the entrance to the kitchen. Her grandmother was standing by herself at the window.

"I knew something was up," Narbie said. "Your grandfather wouldn't tell me that you were with the little ones until just a minute ago. He's in there right now, packing a few things for you."

Helen noted the tears slowly tracing their way down her soft cheeks.

"Ohhh, Grandmother…" Helen ran around the table and into her waiting arms.

"I'm scared for you, sweetie," Narbie finally said, her voice breaking. "Martin's been talking to Pareen and that little friend of yours called Bo. They say trouble has returned, but he won't put a name to it." Narbie gently pushed her to arm's length and looked into her eyes. "Martin's friend, the one called Pareen, speaks to him often. Martin says she lives in the old, Willingham home. For the like of me, I don't remember a single Willingham living near here. But when they are together, Martin, the little ones, and Pareen, they seem to hang on every word the lady says." She paused as she studied Helen for a moment. "What's happening now?" she asked softly.

"Grandmother…" Helen paused, hearing Martin rummaging around in her bedroom. "A lot of this is strange to me also. We are having to deal with a very bad woman. We had a long talk with her a short while ago but it didn't turn out the way we would have liked I'm afraid."

"Am I to be worried, Helen?" Narbie's eyes were still fixed on Helen's.

Helen slowly shook her head. "I don't think so, Grandmother. I believe Grandfather and Pareen have her number."

"Truthfully said," Martin Tucker said.

Helen turned to see him standing at the hallway entrance to the kitchen. Narbie stared at the black, doctor's bag in his right hand and a small suitcase in the other. He was wearing his jacket also.

"I think I have most of what you and I might need in the suitcase. Get your jacket. Bo and his people have the food and supplies for the trip."

"Trip?" Narbie's asked, not bothering to hide her concern or fear. "How long will you be gone and where are you going?"

"Ohhh…" Martin threw a quick glance at Helen. "A day or two, probably. Bo said something about Frank's Crossing I believe."

"Well…" Narbie looked at Helen then back at Martin. "That's straight south of here and down the Whitestone Road. Can you all get into your old MG?"

"Not really," Martin said. "Besides, the Dwarves don't trust something that backfires, smells funny, and smokes like a Dragon. We'll be trying to follow Seleene I believe."

"The wolf?" Narbie's asked.

"Yes, as a matter of speaking," Martin said. "Entwhistle and Dullbriar are following her right now. I believe the wolf has taken them to the Great Beach area. That's north of where Laphidius Monks used to live."

Narbie squinted again. "How do you know this, Martin? Those little people don't have cell phones or the like."

Martin laughed softly. "Entwhistle does. She's taken a liking to mine I believe."

"Entwhistle is in the woods now?" Helen asked.

Martin nodded. "She left with them knowing you would help us."

"Who is this Laphidius Monks person?" Helen asked as she watched her grandfather stuff sausage and biscuits into a paper bag.

"She used to be a very dangerous and powerful Witch in the days of Richard Alvis. She was dispelled, as it were, by his Dragon I am told. Old Alvis' spell will leave us somewhere between Rocky Ford and where we'll have to go."

"Makes little difference," Helen said. "Once this side of the Great Ash, the spell is gone anyway."

"True enough," Martin agreed. "Entwhistle and Dullbriar are now without it also." He paused, looking at Helen. "The old Witch, Monks I mean, left a spell of her own it has been said by Bo. It has some kind of connection with where she once lived, I do believe. We must be very careful once there."

~ * ~

About an hour later, around 9:30 a.m., Helen, Martin, Borack, Bo and Fairweather were heading south on the original Whitestone Road in a wagon supplied by Borack. Pareen and John were on horses and right behind their wagon. Not much more than a one lane, gravel road, it was the only one that led to a place still called the Great Beach Community. Remnants of the old trail still stretched from Maidenhead, past the old Whitestone Castle, and on south toward the Hollow Mountains on the south coast of England. The little group had not traveled far until Bo stopped the horses beneath an old white oak.

"This the place?" Fairweather, looked at Bo.

Bo nodded to his left, toward the east. "Used to be called the Great Beach Community. If you climb that big oak, you'll see Gray Rock in the distance. That's on the north edge of Grassy Lake. This is what Borack calls Grassy Edge." He glanced at Professor Tucker. "The tree we're headin' for is a bit south-east of here. Did you bring the book?"

"I did," Martin replied. "But is the time right?"

Pareen looked at the Professor.

"Yes," Fairweather agreed. "We must bring an end to the Black Witch while she is still in reach."

"What book?" Pareen finally asked Her gaze still locked on the Professor as she reined her horse closer to the wagon.

The Professor looked down at the gravel, glanced at Helen, and then turned to Pereen. "If you had Richard Alvis' Book of Shadows, would you know how to use it?"

Helen's mouth slowly opened as did Pereen's.

"This book still exists?" Pereen asked.

Martin slowly nodded. "It does and by all rights, it should belong to Helen.

"Well said," Bo replied, his smile beaming. "Before all of these here, we would hear you repeat the Master of the Book if you would."

A loud cheer immediately rose up from all the Dwarves ending in applause which the Professor, John, and Pereen gladly joined.

The Professor then pulled a three by ten by twelve-inch-long metal box from the suitcase. Everyone grew quiet, staring at the white feather painted upon the dark green box. 'For the boy,' was written upon the feather in black ink.

Martin looked up at Bo. "Is it time?"

Bo took a long, deep breath. "I suppose so, Professor." He then looked to Pereen. "Two and a half years should have washed the curse from Long Barr I do believe and we are six months or so past that."

Pereen's eyes widened as her fingers slowly found their way to hide her mouth. "Does the book have Richard's words to help Long —a real wizard's spell perhaps?"

"Summons From the Tree," Bo said as the Professor handed Pereen the metal box.

"But…" Fairweather looked back up at Bo. "Can anyone here save Helen say the words and be recognized by the spell itself? He quickly cupped his ears toward Bo.

Pereen slowly opened the box, and gingerly pulled out a large, hard-bound, leather book that looked as old as time itself. The name Alvis was on the front cover. "Helen Durkin," she said loudly. "You are the last in the line of Alvis and this book rightly belongs to you. You are the Master of this Book of Shadows belonging to the Wizard Alvis. I would defend that with her if needs be."

Then, as if someone rang a bell, all eyes looked to Helen.

"This is not fair," Helen grumbled. Her voice very soft. "Everyone is now depending on me. I feel as if I'm being set up to fail."

"Not so My Lady," Fairweather said. Smiling, he leaned closer to her. "None of us can talk ta trees young lass."

The cheer rose again from the Dwarves and quieted just as quick with all eyes again on Helen.

Helen looked to Pereen. "The Druid in the oak protected us against an evil that is no longer here—the Hobuerich.

Bo smiled. "His name is Limbisconn, Helen. I still remember him and as sure as the Dryads are watching, he is also. He spoke at the barn did he not?"

Helen nodded as she looked down and slowly opened the book in her lap. The dry binding cracked as she did so.

"Put it back, Lass," Bo advised. "The chips of parchment lay in the box like cracker crumbs. We'll open it when we get to Pereen's place and the Tree of Sorrows."

"Wouldn't think Ibenus would be—" Bo started.

"We need Long's bow," Fairweather interrupted with a grin

slowly forming under his bushy mustache. "We've been here long enough without his words."

"To the Tree of Sorrows then," Bo said loudly as he snapped the reins.

"What is this 'Tree of Sorrows'? the big woodsman asked.

Pereen's smile widened. "It's another lesson in faith, John. The White Elf within you will understand".

Part 4
Joining of the Once and the Now

Now, with Gray Rock looming over their left shoulder, seven souls left the quest for the Witch and pressed on toward the Tree of Sorrows in hopes of freeing the expert bowman called Long Barr. Bo, constantly distracted by the slightest movement, continually searched the trees for the Great Horned Owl and its rider.

"At least we're goin' in the right direction," Borack grumbled.

"Quit your grumblin'," Fairweather said. "This is all for a good cause and timely as well. Bo's made three arrows tipped with an amethyst head. Long is our best hope to hit the child and not chance killing her. You heard John say that with the witch in her Elisa was much too fast for us. The Professor done ground the Expellax but we got ta get close enough ta dust her with it. Long don't have ta get that close."

"So…" Borack glared back at Pareen from the driver's seat. "We're spendin' valuable time hopein' that a book older than dirt will pry Long Barr from the Tree of Sorrows?"

Bo frowned, gripping the reins tighter. Hardly affording Borack a glance, he replied, "He's not in the tree, ya field fairy. He's up and amongst them somewhere." Bo quickly searched the trees they were passing under.

John slowly shook his head. "I feel like I've took a step back in time here," he grumbled.

Borack immediately laughed, slapping his knee. "Ya have, big fella, and Bo's feather hints at just who is watching us right now."

~ * ~

In little time, Bo led the little group east on the Coon Creek Road once more. A steady breeze stirred the trees. But the clouds, although dark, lacked the size for a serious storm. With but a short time on the Creek Road, they came to the trail leading north to Pereen's house.

Bo slowed the wagon and reined the horses onto the narrow trail. *Something looks different,* he thought, searching up into the limbs of the trees and the sky above him. *That blamed owl is here. I know it is.*

But I think it not a white owl. Is that a good or a bad sign? He brushed his hair back again, reminding himself he still had his cap and feather.

"What's got your goat?" John, looking at Bo, urged his chestnut up close to the wagon seat.

Bo shrugged. "Don't know just yet. Just a feelin' I suppose." He glanced back at Pareen, and then looked at Helen. "Come, let's try that book at the tree. It's where I last saw Long."

So, they continued the short distance to Pereen's house, through the opening in the fence and plumb thicket, and then onto the lower grounds where the old White Oak was. Bo stopped the wagon just outside the reach of its limbs.

Borack stood in the wagon. "Bless my beard," he said weakly, staring at the old tree.

Fairweather, hearing the comment, looked to where his friend was staring. There, not five paces from them, was Bo's moleskin cap hanging from a limb.

Bo's hand immediately went to his head. "Thunderation!" he exclaimed. "When did the horned buzzard get it this time?"

All laughed as Bo eased the horses forward, stood, and snatched his cap from the limb.

"The owl did that?" John.

Laughing, Borack replied, "It was the Dryad atop the beast my rather large friend."

"Come," Bo said as he tied the reins to the wagon's brake handle. "Let's get the ladies started on this."

Fairweather reached across Bo's left shoulder. "Let me have the horses. I'll tie 'em up while you lead 'em all to the tree." He looked to Pereen and John. "Tie your mounts to the wagon. I'll hold 'em still whilst the ladies do what needs be done. There's no tellin' what might happen and the animals might not like it."

Bo looked back at Pereen. She was standing by her horse, looking at the tree as if afraid to get closer than she was already.

"My Lady?" Bo's voice was soft.

Pereen slowly looked to him.

Bo smiled. "Long is more important to you than anyone else in the world. We all know you loved him. I know you have doubts in you being able to read from the book and make it work. Perhaps if you and our Bright Helen both read the words together, it would be helpful."

Helen's smile widened. "I would like that very much," she added, watching Pereen nod slightly.

Then, as all watched, the two walked to within four paces of the trunk of the old oak and knelt in the grass. Pereen slowly opened the box and eyed the old book.

"Page one sixty-two," the Professor prompted.

Pereen gently turned the darkened, parchment pages to the place directed by Professor Martin. Glancing at Helen, she added, "I'm ready when you are."

So, as the others watched, the two read aloud the spell entitled 'Summon From a Tree'.

"In the midst of Bark and wood,
Whether willow, oar, or ash,
I bid thee come to where last you stood,
Where the once and now will clash."

"Holliock!" they both shouted at the end of the spell.

The Professor leaned close to Bo. "What is that word they used?" he whispered.

"Holliock," whispered Bo. "I think it's an ancient word used by wizards long ago. It kind of strengthens an old or seldom used spell."

Then, just as the two were talking, there came a sound so intense it moved the air all around them kicking up a strong breeze from the north. Quick the sound was as if wood on wood triggering the opening of some ancient door, jarring the ground as well as the trees. All sat wide-eyed looking at each other as leaves from the old tree slowly drifted down and all about them.

"The horses," Fairweather said, struggling to hold the wagon team.

"I got 'em!" John ran to aid the old Dwarf.

Helen glanced at Pereen. "Should we stay here?"

"Shhh," the Green Witch hissed. "Help me watch the woods, for I don't believe Long is in the old tree."

"In the tree?" John asked from the wagon.

"Be quiet. Watch and learn," Fairweather advised.

Helen, still sitting in the grass with Pereen, slowly looked about the old tree, then searched the woods around it.

"The breeze has stopped," Pereen whispered.

"There!" Fairweather exclaimed from the wagon.

Looking to where the old Dwarf was pointing, they all spotted a huge, horned owl flying into a nearby ash tree next to the old oak.

"Where'd it go?" Borack asked, now searching the tree with the others.

"Don't know," Bo said. "Disappeared in the leaves and limbs it did."

"There!" John pointed to the bird as it flew from the ash and quickly entered the Tree of Sorrows.

"That owl's got no rider," the big woodsman said.

"I'm no longer sure that's an owl," Borack said. "I'm now thinkin' Bo was right. 'Twas no ordinary owl took his hat. 'Twas Long Barr with it."

The air remained still as everyone searched the old oak for the owl. But then, just as they were about to give up, the stiff breeze came again. It was not from the north this time, but seemed to blow this way and that, causing the old tree to move about boldly, losing many of its leaves as it did. Pereen quickly closed the book, returned it to its metal box, and pulled it to her chest as the leaves swirled violently all around them.

"Look and see!" Helen exclaimed.

"The leaves are moving back into the oak!" Pereen said.

Shielding her face with her hands Pereen looked toward the old tree as a whirlwind began to form in its midst. It slowly moved from the tree and toward the ground between the two and the old oak.

"That's it," Helen said. Pulling Pereen to her feet, the two girls backed away toward the wagon with the others.

But as the whirlwind settled to the ground, it became smaller and smaller, weaker and weaker. When it finally subsided, it left an oblong pile of green, oak leaves seven feet long, four feet wide, and three feet high.

"Bright Child…" The voice sounded like that of a young girl. What's more—it came from between the two, young women."

Helen quickly looked to where Pereen was already staring. There, standing in the grass all of four feet from the two, was a young girl. All of twelve inches tall she was, and smiling up at them both.

Helen smiled. "I know you," she finally managed. "You've helped me at the Yellow Grass and also when the Witch brought the evil faeries."

The little girl straightened her green, leaf-like dress out and smoothed back her sandy-colored hair as best she could. Still in all, it looked as if it was combed by the wind.

The little Druid looked at Pereen. "Daughter of Eefron," she stated with a slight bow. She then turned to Helen. Her blue eyes sparkled like spring water in the sun. "Bright Helen, you two have proved worthy. Your actions, both past and now, have shown me your heart. My name is Colleene," she added, fiddling with her hair again. "Do you remember how the Dwarf called the Fae when Seleene was tracking you?"

Helen nodded. "He shaved the bark from an old oak, placed his hand upon the moist, green wood and then recited a poem."

Coleen quickly looked at Bo.

Bo quickly bowed. "My lady of the Oak. I will teach her The Words of Calling."

Colleene nodded and then looked back to Pereen. "Do the same for the Daughter of Eefron if you will."

"Consider it done," Bo said.

The Druid then looked to the pile of green leaves, hardly thirty feet away. "We will leave the one called Long Barr with you now. He will be thirsty, weak, and hungry. Tend to that immediately if you will."

"We will, My Lady," Bo said with another, slight bow.

"Ohhh God…" Pereen crumpled to the grass with her head in her hands.

Helen immediately knelt beside her. Slipping her left arm over Pereen's shoulder, she gave her a gentle hug.

Colleene looked back, smiling at Helen. "Limbisconn has allowed us to take him from the wood. He will need clothing."

Not waiting for a reply, the Dryad flew from them. Hovering ten feet above the pile of leaves, she commanded, "Return to the tree! He is in good hands!"

All of a sudden, and almost faster than the eye could follow, the leaves seemed to come to life. Swirling about the lifeless body now lying upon the grass, they streaked back up into the limbs above and disappeared.

"I got this!" Borack raced forward with a brown, cloth bag. From it, he pulled a long, green robe and laid it over his friend.

"I've got you," John said softly as he scooped Pereen up in his arms and walked toward Long Barr with the others close behind. "I can't believe what I've just seen," he whispered as he gently sat her in the grass beside Long Barr.

Wiping the tears from her eyes, she looked up at John. "I'm having trouble with it myself. Pereen leaned closer to Long Barr. "He looks so cold and pale." But as she said those words, she watched his eyes move under his lids. "Long..." Her voice was soft as she gently touched his forearm.

Flinching from her touch, his eyes began to flutter wildly. "Where am I?" His voice weak as he continued to blink.

"You're back with us, Long," Pereen said. "It's been three years."

"I know that voice." Long tried to sit up. Failing that, he slowly laid back in the grass with his eyes shut. "Pereen?" His left hand searched for hers.

Gently taking it, she pulled it to her chest. "You're back with us, Long." Her eyes welled up again. "Can you see?"

"Here..." The Professor rummaged through his bag. Quickly producing a small, plastic bottle, he handed it to Pereen. "Just squeeze it and let the solution drip into his eyes. It's just a saline solution. It won't hurt him if you use it all."

In doing that, Pereen watched him bat his eyes wildly.

"Everything looks so bright," Long said still blinking his eyes. "Only shadows I now see."

"Bandage his eyes for now," the Professor said as he handed Pereen a roll of white gauze. "They'll be fine, Long," he added. "We don't want you to strain them right now."

"Thank you." Long started to get up, but then grabbed at the robe. "I guess my clothes didn't make it back did they?"

"They did not," Borack said as he stepped closer. "But I got most of what you'll need."

Long propped himself up on his left elbow as Pareen finished bandaging his eyes.

"Borack?" Long asked.

"The same," the Dwarf replied. "Can you stand?"

After Pareen finished tying the bandage, the Professor took Long's right arm around his own shoulders and with John's help, hoisted the weak halfling to his feet.

"What was it like ta be an Int?" Fairweather asked, stepping closer and cupping his ears toward the answer.

"Fair? Is that you?" Long asked, gripping Pereen's hand.

"It is that, and we have Bright Helen, the Professor, Bo, and John all with us."

Long paused, turning toward where the old Dwarf had spoken. "I don't know a John."

Laughter rose up again with applause from the Dwarves.

"He's a friend," Pareen explained. "He's someone you'll have to see to believe—a White Elf."

Long smiled. "A White Elf? Imagine that." He turned toward Pereen. "Did we lose anyone? I mean…"

"The Dryads saved us Long," Pereen answered. "They ran the Hobuerich off as well as helped me with Ibenus. But, as Fate would have it, we are after the Black Witch again. She is still with us. Now, answer Fair's question— 'What's it like being an Int?'"

"Int?" Long paused. "Not sure I was ever one," he finally answered. "At times, I think I could see the old Druid's face— Limbisconn I mean. Most of it was like a dream—never got hungry, never got thirsty, never worried about anything—that is, as long as I stayed in the trees. Later, the Dryads taught me how to venture away from them. That was very different. It was like I weighed nothing— riding on the slightest breeze, relishing the occasional rainstorm, or even flying with the great raptors." He laughed. "I even got hungry. Sorry it took so long. I had no sense of time at all."

He reached up to John's shoulder to steady himself as he sat back in the grass. Finding it well above his head, he reached for the bandage to better see the man helping him.

"Forget that," Pereen scolded with a gentle slap to his hand. "That stays on until the Professor says different."

"That's our John Schmidt," Bo said, steadying Long's right arm as he sat back down in the grass. "You'll meet him soon enough."

Long nodded and then turned toward the sound of Bo's voice. "Sorry 'bout the hat, Bo. I was aware of the Druid's intentions and just wanted to keep you headed in my direction."

"No harm done," Bo replied. "After all, how many can boast of a Dryad feather in their cap?"

John leaned closer. "You moved about very much, or perhaps followed those you knew?"

"At times I tried to be heard," Long said. "But, try as I did, I could never gain anyone's attention. While among the trees, I would just think of a place—at the top of the tree, at the end of a limb, or at its trunk. I could move there very quickly, even to other nearby trees as long as they were oaks, ashes, beeches or the occasional willow. But when I was out of the tree, it was very different. Where before, I could hardly feel anything. Once out, I could then feel the slightest breeze, the warmth of the sun, and the fresh rain was like a fine desert to me. My sense of smell had also returned." He looked toward Bo, gripping his hand also. "While out and flying through the night skies, I developed quite a taste for rabbits, and your hat when my memory allowed me to recall my friends." Slowly looking toward Pereen he added, "But I never forgot the one I loved."

"Ah hah!" Borack exclaimed, slapping his knee. "You were with an owl weren't you?"

"Yes," John replied. "The Dryads would always bring me one."

Pereen smiled as her face grew warm. "It took you three months to visit me in my dreams, but I saw the Great Horned owl quite frequently."

Long nodded. "I suppose the word 'time' doesn't exist where I was allowed to stay. Have you got water?"

"Get him drink and food," Bo ordered, sending Fairweather and Borack scrambling toward the wagon bed.

~ * ~

Shortly after 1:00 p.m., and with a freshly added member, the little group was back on the original Whitestone Trail and heading south. With no plan at all on how to find the witch, their hopes were now on whatever Entwhistle, Dullbriar, the Corgi Zee, and the timber wolf Seleene could turn up. Long Barr, resting as best he could in the wagon, eyed what Bo had laid next to him—his bow, quiver, and axe. With his head and shoulders in Pereen's lap, and the Professor on her horse, he was as content as possible in the rough-riding wagon.

"How's your peepers?" Fairweather asked, smiling at Long Barr.

"Not real sure. At least they don't hurt right now."

Helen looked up at Bo in the wagon seat. "Can we make him a wet poultice and press it against the bandages. The moisture will do him well." She glanced at the Professor to see him nod his head.

Then, as Helen scrambled to find water and cloth, The Professor's cell phone rang. Bo immediately slowed the wagon to a stop as all looked toward Martin.

Immediately stopping his mount, the Professor hurriedly took out his phone. "Hello," he said, finally finding it. Listening for a minute or so, he looked to Bo. "Does the old mound north of Frank's Crossing mean anything to anyone?"

"Yes," Fairweather answered, not waiting for his brother. "That's where old Laphidius Monks used to live. There's a crystal stone with a black streak through it where she's buried."

"Three hours from here at best," Bo added.

"We're coming, Entwhistle," the Professor said. "Be patient. It'll take about three hours or so." Putting the phone back in his jacket, he turned to Bo. "She said Seleene has found John's daughter but she is acting very unusual."

Borack stared at the Professor. "Isn't that where Laphidius is buried?"

"The Professor nodded with "Quite near it."

~ * ~

A little over an hour into the journey, Bo slowed the wagon to a stop. The topography had changed dramatically with the hardwoods and pines thinning, pampas grass, cattails, and willows now abounded with the hardier evergreens. While noticing the occasional creek before, those had given way to standing water and marshy places.

"What's the problem," Fairweather asked, rising to his knees in the wagon.

Bo glanced back. "Gossamer Swamp," came the quick reply.

The old Dwarf slowly sank back to the hardwood wagon bed. "No Dwarf likes this place," he grumbled. "Used to be the eastern part of Black Forest. Back in old Alvis's day, it consumed things that wandered into it." He looked at Bo in the wagon seat. "Ya think this place holds the spell that is rumored to exist from the dead witch?"

"Not good!" Long tugged at his bandages as he tried to sit up.

"Down with you," Pereen ordered as she stopped his hand from pulling at the gauze.

"We shouldn't worry," Pereen said. "She wasn't as powerful as our Richard and his last spell is truly fading."

John slowly shook his head. "I fear I'm at a loss here, my

friends. He looked to Fairweather.

The old Dwarf smiled. "In the old days, people, Dwarves, and Elves would go in and sometimes not come out, never to be heard from again." He slowly looked about the place. "What's more—I believe we've lost old Alvis' spell."

Borack stood from the wagon seat and looked about the place also. "I feel it. Queer it is. Every hair on the back of my neck is standin' up right now."

"Yea," Fairweather agreed. "Goosebumps too."

"But we shouldn't stop right now," Pereen said with a grumble. "This Black Forest/Gossamer thing faded away years ago. The Tomes of Records say as much. There were four powerful witches who lived here and were tolerated by an equally evil wizard. Richard Alvis and his Dragon Pragamore dealt with them, but not entirely. Before that end came about, the witches destroyed the greater part of a nearby community by casting a spell. That's how the Gossamer Swamp came into existence and that's what has Bo stopped right now."

"The Swamp itself?" John asked.

"No-no-no," Long interrupted, trying to resist Pereen's hand. "The spell didn't kill the townspeople. It turned 'em into water hags. That's how those unlucky ones disappeared. They were preyed upon by those that lived here...or still live here."

"Heavens..." Helen looked at Bo. He was standing still as a post in the wagon and looking down the makeshift, stone road through the swamp.

"Hey..." Borack nudged Bo. "We need to get to Frank's Crossing. Starin' at the swamp ain't gon'na make it go away you know."

Bo barely afforded him a glance. "I've read the 'Tomes of Time'," he said weakly. "In them is set the history of our people. Isn't it strange to you that of all places this is the one that has been all but left out? And now, here we are. Every hair on my arms is standin' on end and I want to grab my axe."

Broderick scratched his head. "We could cut east and through the woods to the paved road."

"Ohhh, that's a great idea," Fairweather grumbled. "We don't have the wizard's spell or the Professor's smelly old vehicle. Wouldn't we look just dandy trottin' down a modern highway in the wagon and on horses? I will not put my people in the path of those who do not understand us or even want to try."

"This is our path." Pereen pointed down the rocky road. The witch is that way and our people are waiting for us right now."

"Pardon me." John urged his horse up beside Bo and looked down at him and Borack. "I know I'm an outsider here my friends, but I've been listenin' in on your conversations. Perhaps I'm not knowledgeable enough to be fearful of this place but it takes a lot ta scare me. If you would permit, I would like to take the point and proud to."

"Well you're wrong, my rather large Elfling," Fairweather said with a chuckle. "You're not an outsider. You're a halfling just like Long and our Bright Helen and the closest one we have to an Elf at this time. Lead on."

Watching John urge his big horse onto the rock road, Bo leaned close to Borack. "A man will lead where a Dwarf would not?"

Borack grinned. "How 'bout an Elf?"

Bo slowly shook his head and snapped the reins.

Borack watched the lead as the wagon slowly rumbled over the rough stones. "Biggest horse I ever saw," he said just above a whisper.

Long Barr propped himself up and looked toward the wagon seat. "He's an Elf?"

Pereen smiled, heeling her mount closer to the wagon.

"He's from Phagan's Rift—last of the White Elves."

"Halfling?" Long squinted. "I'd hate to see a whole one."

All the Dwarves laughed as the wagon rumbled over the rocky crossing.

Now, led by a friend of the Green Witch, the topography began to change again. Dead hardwoods and pines gave way to the hardier cypress. Swamp grass and ferns were now taking the place of knee-high grass and the brambles of the forest. But the water remained remarkably clear, supplied by numerous small creeks from the higher grounds skirting what they could still see of the forest. Waterfowl and egrets fluttered here and there lending more positive opinions of the place. Colorful five-inch Dragon flies, busy tapping their tails on the water's surface, seemed to ignore them completely.

John looked back at the wagon, now only a few yards away. "These Water Hag things, what do they look like?"

"Hopefully dead," Borack said. His face stern. "Should of

volunteered to go with Entwhistle."

Fairweather laughed. "According to the Tomes, they are hooked-nosed, hump-backed, snaggle toothed, skinny beings who remain more comfortable in the water than out."

John raised his eyebrows as he slowly turned forward. "Maybe them siblings didn't make it at all," he added weakly.

Less than two miles the Rocky Road stretched through what remained of Gossamer Swamp. But after the first mile, small islands of land began to appear here and there with hardy cypress and evergreens.

"See…" Fairweather still laughing at those jaded. "The swamp's changin'. The water's still clear as the creeks that feed it. Don't be spooked by what used to—"

"Hold!" John shouted, cutting off the old Dwarf.

Seeing John had stopped, Bo pulled back on the reins and quickly stood. "What's got your goa—"

Bo's comment froze on his tongue as he looked past John. Forty yards or so past him, and standing on the twenty-foot wide road, stood the huge wolf.

"Helen, get up here." Bo called, trying to be as quiet as the moment would allow. "I think we just found Seleene, but I don't see anyone else around at all."

Fairweather, now standing behind Bo and Borack, laughed at the big woodsman. "Haven't ya been followin' the beast? Didn't think she made you nervous."

John glanced back toward the wagon. "She tolerated me. At times, it was like she wanted me to follow."

"Uh huh…" Borack leaned to the left, looking around John and the big draft. "It has not moved. Don't see Entwhistle, Dullbriar, or Zee."

John glanced back again. "Was not the wolf supposed to be followin' my daughter?"

Long Barr sat up, tugging at his bandages.

Allow him," the Professor said.

"Let me help." Pereen quickly loosened the knot behind his head.

Slowly taking them off, Long rubbed his eyes, looking at Pereen.

"Can you see me?" she asked softly.

"Blue eyes and all," Long Barr replied as he stood behind the wagon seat, gently rubbing his eyes. Grabbing his axe, he put it in his belt, and then looked to Pereen. She was holding up to him the bow and quiver.

"Can ya see 'em," Fairweather asked, pointing past John.

Long nodded, gripping the bow. "Clear enough to hit him."

Bo looked back at him. "Let's not just yet. I think she's workin' for us right now."

"Wasn't she supposed to be followin' John's daughter?" Came again the question as Fairweather also stood in the wagon.

Helen climbed over the edge of the wagon and started walking toward John.

The Professor noted she wasn't slowing as she approached the woodsman. "Helen, that's far enough," he called as he watched Seleene begin to trot toward her.

"Look there, past the woodsman," Fairweather said, pointing toward two mounted figures well past Seleene.

Long eased from the wagon with his bow. "Were not these trying to find the witch?" He looked back to the Professor. "Do you still have your wee pistol?"

"No need for that," Pereen advised. "We're here to rescue John's daughter, not harm her."

Suddenly, a shrill scream echoed across the swamp, to their left, and toward the paved highway almost a mile away. As it sounded, Seleene stopped and looked toward a narrow piece of land that extended toward them from that direction. The dry tip of it was a good thirty yards away from the crossing.

"Hold that," John said, noting Long was rubbing his eyes with arrow in hand. He slowly looked toward the jetty. "That don't sound like my Elisa at all."

"Not particularly pleased with it myself," Borack, nervously tapping his sheathed axe with his right hand.

Temporarily distracted by the scream, the Professor looked back to his granddaughter. She had passed John and was continuing toward Seleene.

"Hold there, Professor Tucker," Bo said. "Our Bright Helen knows what she's doin' with the wolf. Those ridin' toward us are my daughter and Dullbriar. They have slowed but are not shoutin' words of caution."

Zee, the corgwn gift to Helen by the Faeries of Kiendom,

quickly left Entwhistle and Dullbriar and ran toward them. Slowing just enough to make eye contact with Seleene, he continued toward Helen. Helen immediately knelt and hugged the orange and white corgwn. At that exact moment, another scream came again, distracting everyone.

"Bo, with us!" Dullbriar shouted.

Looking in that direction, Bo noticed the wolf had darted past Dullbriar and Entwhistle and was now heading for where the rocky road ended at a dead run.

"In the wagon," Fairweather said, glancing at Long Barr. "She's out for the Black Witch again."

"Where're we goin?" John asked as Bo reined the wagon around the big draft.

"To kill a witch, my friend," an excited Bo answered.

Part 5
To Kill a Witch

Once off the Rocky Ford, the woods quickly began to look a lot better to Bo. The huge trees lent him a sense of safety, somehow, and the hags were off of his mind. The trail gradually turned more west and toward the paved highway. Pereen, Helen, and the Dwarves continually searched the shadows of the forest even though the wolf had already passed through them. The horrible scream lay heavy upon their minds.

Helen stood, holding to the back of the wagon seat. "Does anyone see the wolf?"

"Nope," quickly answered Bo, snapping the reins again. "I can see Entwhistle and Dullbriar. They're not that far ahead of us and stayin' on the trail thus far."

"We're getting close to the Crystal Mound where Laphidius is buried," said Pereen.

Borack slowly shook his head as he held to the side of the wagon seat. "There's that name again. I hate Black Witches," he grumbled. "The hair on the back of my neck has been standin' on end ever since that last scream."

"And now one is leadin' us to where the worst of 'em is buried," Fairweather added.

Helen nudged Bo. "Did the Wizard Richard Alvis kill her? She glanced at Pereen.

"Not exactly," Bo said, "but he was the reason she died. "That is to say; he wasn't the actor in that particular drama."

Helen looked at Pereen, then Bo, and back at Pereen again. "May I know the one responsible for her death?"

"Not sure." Pereen's voice was low. "I don't want to cause any more trouble for that one in his last days."

Helen, completely unaware of what the Green Witch had just hinted at, watched Fairweather's eyes grow big and look away from the group.

"Bless my beard," the old Dwarf exclaimed. His comment was so loud it caused everyone to look back at him. Bo pulled back on the reins, stopping the wagon so fast everyone in it had to catch themselves on the side panels.

Long quickly sat up, looking at him also. "Did she say—"

"Yes!" Fairweather said. "She did!"

"Ohhh…" Pereen groaned as she looked up at the white clouds.

Fairweather's countenance quickly grew as troubled and dark as a thunderstorm. "Just like an elf! Keep the proof of our past in the world of men where we would have no idea of—"

"Calm down," Bo ordered. "They can hear you all the way to the paved highway."

John wheeled his draft around so quick it left the Professor in the lead. "Do we have a problem?" he asked as he rode up to the wagon. He looked straight at Fairweather. The Dwarf's expression unchanged.

Fairweather's intense stare drifted from John and ended up on Pereen. "The Dragon Pragamore killed the Witch Laphidius Monks. He perceived her to be a threat to the House of Alvis. At that particular time, Richard was a very young wizard about the same age as our Bright Helen. The Green Witch has stumbled and I have caught her." He stared at Pereen. "Where is Richard's Dragon now?"

Bo looked back at Pereen. "Please answer his question."

"He's in good hands," John said. His gaze was locked on Fairweather.

Fairweather's gaze lowered to the wagon bed. "And how am I to judge that?" he grumbled.

"By the mere fact that he still lives," Pereen said, her tone vexed. She paused to regain her composure as the Professor rode back to join them.

"What's happening?" the Professor asked, noting the anger of the moment.

"Later," Fairweather said. He sat back down hard in the wagon bed.

The Professor looked at Pereen. "What shook his tree? I could hear him all the way up to the point."

"Lack of trust as he sees it," Pereen answered. "He found out that the Pan's son still lives."

"What?" The Professor's chin slowly dropped. "Pandar's son is still alive? The Dragon Pragamore still lives?"

"All of those," John quipped, a bit humored at the Professor's astounded expression.

"Uhhh…" Pereen groaned, looking up from beside Long Barr. "If I had wings, this is where I would fly away."

Long smiled. "That is, after all, a huge secret to be kept for so long," he said softly. "You should try to smooth this over somehow and quickly. I am a halfling myself, but Bo, Fairweather, Dullbriar, and Borack are not. Being continually razzed by Elves in the past, we should try to keep that kind of thing in the past."

"Professor!"

The shout came from up ahead on the trail. Everyone looked to see Dullbriar approaching at a gallop. "We have company," he said as he rode up.

Everyone stopped, and started looking about the woods all around them.

"Don't think you'll see 'em," Dullbriar said. "Entwhistle knows this fellow, but his name doesn't ring any bells in my memory."

"What's his name?" asked Bo.

"Donder Franks." Dullbriar stared at the others, searching for a sign of recognition.

"I think I know who you're speakin' of," Fairweather replied. "A little older than Helen and a bit tall for a Dwarf?"

Dullbriar nodded.

Fairweather smiled. "If I'm right, that's a halfling who's mother died of a fever some years ago. Her name was Tawny Pennyworth and a Dwarf. She married a man. Franks was his name," he continued as he stood in the wagon. "Seems ta me there was a rift of some kind twixt the Dwarves and this man after she died and he was banished from Leachenwood. I believe he ended up living in a place just east of there." Fairweather squinted at Dullbriar. "Why do ya think he's here right now?"

"Entwhistle," Dullbriar said. "She said he was helping her with Seleene."

Long Barr handed his cool water poultice to Helen. "I wouldn't worry about him. He's a halfling like me. He's probably not that sure about us right now."

"You certain?" Borack asked.

"Whatever." Long Barr grumbled as he jumped from the wagon. "I'm a five-foot, six-inch Dwarf and you trust me don't ya?"

"Long…" Pereen held the poultice out for him.

"I'm fine. Vision is back and everything." He stretched his back, grimacing. "I've just got to get this stiffness worked out of me. Do we have anything to eat without making a fuss?"

"Big, wooden box," Bo said, looking back from the wagon seat. "There's jerky, dried plums and apples."

Long looked to Pereen. "I'll take whatever you get to first."

As Long was eating what Pereen found, Dullbriar cleared his throat loudly, gaining their attention. "I think he's here. Look up ahead where the trail forks to the left. He and Entwhistle are there already. She just handed him something wrapped in linen."

Long turned around, looking at the others and noticed Dullbriar slip back onto the woods. "Where has Dullbriar slipped off to?"

Bo, looking also, replied, "Hopefully, he's checkin' this fellow out. I'm not fond of secrets and my daughter is lousy with 'em right now. I'm wondering what she handed that stranger."

Bo, handed the reins to Borack, got out of the wagon with Fairweather and started walking toward the two at the fork. As they did, the one called Donder turned and walked away into the woods.

"Speakin' of secrets," Long grumbled. "What do you make of that?" He glanced back at the wagon and signaled them to follow.

Bo silently shook his head as they walked up to Entwhistle. "Do we have a plan most of us are not aware of?"

"Uhhh…" She glanced at Fairweather.

"Look at me!" Bo shouted. His face red with anger. "We just had a flamin' argument about secrets and yet, here we are again. Am I not the head of this little party?"

"Yes," Entwhistle said. "At least the Dwarf part of it."

"Is that Donder Franks?" Bo asked as Fairweather got out of the wagon.

"He is," Entwhistle said, almost looking down her nose at her father. "And that last argument has a lot to do with what's gon'na happed next I believe."

"What's gon'na happen?" Bo's scowl deepened. "Here we are again. The argument was concerning the Dragon and I'm still in the dark!"

Entwhistle grimaced, glancing at Fairweather.

Fairweather placed his left hand lightly on Bo's right shoulder.

"Calm down a bit, Bo. Don has two of the amethyst arrows and—"

At that very instant, Dullbriar came running up from the woods. Completely out of breath, he bent over and braced himself with his hands on his knees. "There's a…" He coughed, trying to catch his breath.

"Bring the wagon close!" Bo shouted. "We need water here and quick."

Borack snapped the reins and guided the wagon team up close to them. Joined by Helen and John, all stood watching as Long handed Dullbriar a metal cup filled with water.

The Dwarf quickly downed it and then walked to the side of the wagon where the wooden water keg was tied, filled the empty cup, and drank again. Slowly turning toward those watching, he managed, "I saw it. I saw it." He turned for another cup of water.

Bo quickly stepped forward. Snatching the cup from the younger Dwarf, he growled, "If ya don't tell us what ya saw, I'll drown you in that water keg."

"Yes Sir," Dullbriar said, still quite shaken. "It's with that man —the one who Entwhistle knows."

"He's not a man," Entwhistle corrected.

"Bless my bunions!" Bo said, glaring at Dullbriar. "If you don't name this 'It' I'll comb your hair with the blade of my axe!"

"All right—all right," Dullbriar managed. "He pointed toward the west. "He's up ahead and two hills over just past the Crystal Mound. Just sittin' there with Bitterthorn and not makin' a sound."

For one, silent moment, all eyes were on Dullbriar. Then, as quick as a cat's sneeze, Bo grabbed his axe and the young Dwarf's collar.

"It's a Dragon!" Dullbriar said, "A Dragon—a huge, greenish-brown Dragon. That Donder fellow and Bitterthorn were there with him. I swear it and I've not been anywheres close to a jug."

Slipping his axe back in his belt, Bo slowly turned and squinted at his daughter. "What are you and this Donder fellow fixin' ta try?"

"Get rid of the witch I hope," Entwhistle said. "We just need you to draw her from the child and get her in the open. Seleene remains close to the…" she looked at John, "…your daughter. The witch is still in her."

John dismounted, as did the Professor.

"You're not going to harm her are you?" John's brow creased

with worry.

"Pragamore will not harm either while the witch is still in your daughter," someone said from the far side of the wagon.

All eyes slowly turned to see the man that just moments ago all were guessing at. Dressed in tawny deerskin pants and shirt, Donder stood smiling at them. No hat, sandy-colored hair to his shoulders, he had an Elfin, white wood bow slung over his right shoulder. He walked around the team and approached them with his left hand resting upon the stone handle of his short sword.

John leaned heavily against the left side of the wagon. "Dwarves, witches, and now Dragons," he said weakly. He briskly rubbed his face with both hands. With his gaze resting on Pereen, he added, "You're the leader of this little parade. Will my daughter get out of this in one piece?"

"I think so," Donder answered.

"Think?" John glared at the halfling.

Donder quickly held his hands up as to stop the big man before he started. "The Witch Ibenus is in her right now, my big friend. What damage that has done is not clear to anyone at this time." He glanced at Bo and then Fairweather. "What is clear to me is that Pragamore is the last Dragon I know of, and he can destroy her no matter what form she takes or where she seeks shelter." He looked back at John as he pulled one of the amethyst tipped arrows from his quiver. "This has to be put under the girl's skin as safely as possible." He then looked to Long Barr. Holding three fingers up, he asked, "How many fingers do you see?"

Long's gaze lowered to the grass between the two. "You've made your point," he replied weakly. "But how is an old Dragon gon'na pull this off?"

Donder smiled, glancing at Pereen and John. "First of all things, my long bow friend, is symbiotic Dragons do-not-lie. He just said he needs to be close to the witch when the arrow strikes her."

Borack looked to Bo. "Getting Ibenus in the open is not gon'na be easy. How are we to make that happen."

"Seleene and Pragamore are two hills south-east of us," Donder explained. "John's daughter is one hill north-west of them. The Dwarf Bitterthorn is watching Pragamore and Pragamore is watching the black witch. The Dragon has made his nest almost atop the second hill and can see the valley where Ibenus has sway over

Elisa. The witch is in full view of the Crystal Mound. So don't go in there without a plan to draw her into the open."

Bo stepped closer to Donder. "Bitterthorn is young and green as grass juice. He knows little of witches."

"He knows enough to be scared," Donder countered. "He was with you on your last encounter with Ibenus. He'll do fine I believe."

"Well…" Fairweather grumbled. "We're down to it aren't we?"

Bo nodded and then looked to Helen. "Bright Lady, are you up to facin' the witch again?"

Helen glanced at her grandfather and then swallowed hard. "I suppose so," she finally answered.

"Very well then." Bo turned to Donder. "Work yourself into the trees this side of where Laphidius's crystal stone rises from the grass in front of the mound. I believe the black witch will approach from the blind side of the mound. Go now."

"I will do my best," Donder said and off he went at a trot.

~ * ~

Thirty minutes later, and about as dark as 8:00 p.m., could get, Bo, Borack, Helen, Long Barr, Dullbriar, Entwhistle, the Professor, and the Corgi Zee eased on toward the mound with John and Pereen on horseback. Now, the shadows of the trees were completely eaten by the dark of the forest.

Helen eased up behind Bo now sitting in the wagon seat. "We do have a plan don't we?" she whispered. Waving the air from her face, she moved back a little. "You smell of whisky," she said, squinting. "This is no time to confuse one's senses."

He looked back at her, smiled, and then replied, "Ibenus will smell it also. I haven't had a drop. Something has to be done to make her think she has the upper hand," Bo whispered, glancing at the others now close also. "I'll go in with you and make a fire about thirty feet this side of the crystal stone. While I'm doing that, you get the beef and meat sticks from the yellow and red Igloo. It has cubes of iced down beef in it. The wagon will remain out of sight. Pay no attention to how I act. Just look a bit irritated, but tolerant. Perhaps she'll take advantage of the situation. She hates us both you know. Hopefully, Donder will get his shot when he sees Pragamore approaching."

~ * ~

Ten minutes later, Bo pulled the wagon in to a well wooded part of the forest within sight of the Crystal Mound. Everyone got out of the wagon or dismounted save Bo and Helen who were now in the wagon seat. Without further discussion, Bo eased the Shelties toward the clearing at the Mound. As they approached, Helen got her first look at the crystal stone the Dwarves of Leachenwood had placed. Eight feet high, twenty inches thick, and four feet across, it stood with a slight lean toward the mound. It was perfectly clear save for the black streak that started in the grass and continued to the very top of the stone.

Helen stood, looking at the crystal. "You say that black streak means she was bad?"

"No, child..." Bo struggled to get out of the wagon. Accomplishing that, he looked back at Helen. "Means she died bad. Weren't always that way I am told. When young, she worked as a midwife and studied herbs, roots, poisons, and the like." His voice loud. "Now, let's build a nice fire and cook us somethin' to eat. I'm starvin'."

Making his steps look unsteady, he gathered firewood and kindling until he had an ample amount for a large fire. As Helen watched him closely, she rummaged for the food sticks and meat in the Igloo. At the same time, she watched toward the hill, its top, and both sides. There was no sign of movement at all.

Fifteen minutes later, and with a crock jug of whiskey, Bo was on his hands and knees, nursing little flames into big ones. Helen eased up beside the crock, uncorked it, and filled the cup half full. Waiting until Bo moved back from the wood, she dashed the cup's contents on what flames were available.

"Whoaaa!" the Dwarf yelled, sitting back hard in the grass. Patting his smoldering beard, he glared at the young girl.

"Sorry," she managed. "I didn't think that stuff was so—"

"Tis all right, Lass." Bo's voice low. "If she didn't know we were here, she does now. Lit up every tree in a hundred yards in either direction it did." He quickly placed more small limbs on the fire.

"I heard the talk of the Dragon," Helen said. Her voice at a whisper. "It really exists then?"

Bo rested back in the grass on one elbow, watching Helen slip the sharpened cooking sticks into the meat. "It, Lass?" Bo corrected. "His name is Pragamore and he's older than all of our ages put together. The Tome states he was the Wizard Alvis's Dragon. That being said, he's the only one here who has actually talked to the Wizard Richard Alvis. So…when, and if, you get to talk to him, speak to him as you would any other person."

"He talks?" Helen's mouth slowly opened as she stared at Bo.

Bo chuckled, slapping his knee. "You're chasin' a witch with a bunch of Dwarves and three halflings. What makes Pragamore so hard to swallow?" Dwarf kept his voice low. He fidgeted with the cork in the crock.

"Seems a bit much." Helen stuck the first meat stick into the ground and leaned the beef close to the flame. "It's kind of like any minute now Ill wake up and this will all be a fantastic dream or something."

Bo placed his finger in the crock's round handle, rolled it on top of his right elbow, and tilted the opening toward his lips. Holding it a bit too long in that position, Helen noticed he wasn't drinking, but looking toward the top of the mound.

"Congratulations," spoke someone from the mound. The voice sounded young, but cynical none the less.

Helen froze with a meat stick in each hand. She slowly searched the darkness atop the mound. "Bo?" she managed weakly.

"Place your sticks, Lass," the Dwarf said as he corked the jug and sat it back in the grass. "I see her," he whispered. "At the near edge of the mound. Watch her glow in the fire's light." He threw more wood upon the fire, sending Helen to readjust the meat sticks.

Helen searched the top of the hill some twenty-five yards away or so and finally caught the shimmering, yellow form that held the Dwarf's attention. She slowly stood with the Dwarf.

The witch laughed, and then spoke. "Your little, meddling group overcame the fae's circle of daffodils and rescued the Green Witch from the Tree of Sorrows where I intended her to stay. That had a cost. Long Barr paid that, but your Green Witch bested that curse also didn't she? Then, you managed to take him from the tree of Sorrows also." She laughed, loud and maniacally, causing Helen to drop a meat stick into the fire. "Tell me, Billy Bo Bumpus, where is the Green Witch now?"

"She is elsewhere," Helen answered, as she and Bo stepped

slightly away from the glare of the fire.

"Bright Helen," she giggled wildly, "the one who talks to trees. Do you think the Int will protect you yet again? He hasn't been heard from in a good-long-while."

The distance to the crystal stone was about thirty feet, and a good ten yards more to the base of the mound. But Helen could easily see the round, glowing face of what looked to be a young girl at its top.

Bo looked down at the fire and whispered. "I fear the lad cannot see her well enough to shoot," he whispered. "We must get her closer."

Helen slowly stepped to the right side of the fire. "Come down that we may see you plainly and discuss what would bring an end to all of this," she said loudly.

"End!" The shadowy figure stepped from the edge of the hill and seemed to slide down its side without moving her feet. "Your grandfather's death would be a start," she added calmly as she slowly walked toward the crystal marker.

"Ohhh geeze," Helen groaned, seeing her pause at the stone.

The events that followed the Witch's next step toward them from the stone were difficult for Helen to follow. She heard the hiss of Donder's arrow as it streaked from the darkness on her right. Elisa's, or rather the witch's scream, was so loud it made Helen jump with her gaze glued to the shaft now protruding from the young girl's left hip. With Elisa's eyes tightly closed, the young girl screamed again as she seized the shaft with her left hand. But before she could do another thing, the top of the hill seemed to come to life. Something greenish-brown, and the size of a small plane shot from it and headed silently toward Elisa, still struggling with the arrow. Completely bowling the young girl forward, the creature's huge hand pushed her body headlong to the grass and completely covered her like a great horned owl would a mouse.

"Nooo!" John screamed as he ran from the shadows behind the Bo and the fire.

But before the big woodsman made it even with Bo; Borack and Bitterthorn tackled him to the ground.

Undaunted by the happenings near her, Helen watched as the Dragon pinned his captive to the ground, watching her closely. Then, as all watched, Elisa let out a single scream and everything grew strangely silent. John, now holding the two Dwarves at bay, looked toward his daughter with tears streaming down his face.

Suddenly, as if the Dragon had what he came for, it leaped from the small girl, bounded into the night air, and then disappeared into the darkness like it had never existed.

"Help me!" John begged as he, Dullbriar, and Borack raced toward the lifeless body of the big woodsman's daughter.

Shocked at the size and the very existence of such a mythical creature, Helen stood frozen in place and stared at the full moon. But the shape she strained to see never came again. She finally shut her mouth, looked toward those now gathering at Elisa's side, and then slowly walked toward them.

"Father…" Elisa seemed to be crying as John sat her up in the grass. "I've been shot! I've been shot!"

"Give me room," Pereen ordered as she pushed by Dullbriar and Borack to kneel beside the young girl. She quickly put her right hand upon the girl's forehead. Elisa immediately passed out in her father's arms. "Professor!" she called.

"Right here," Martin said. Kneeling beside John, the Professor rummaged through his black bag. Glancing at Donder, he asked, "Flesh wound, but not real deep thank God. What shape is the arrow's head?"

"There are no wings, Professor," Donder answered. "It should pull right out without tearing the flesh."

"Yes. Well…" The Professor looked back at Helen. "Prepare me a poultice bandage with plenty of Neosporin. There's a partially used tube in the bag. But first, get me a clean rag. I've got a bottle of alcohol in the bag." He looked at John. "Hold her tight, my friend. This won't feel good and she's liable to awaken."

In less than a minute, Helen was back with a hand towel and quickly produced the bottle of alcohol.

"Ready?" Martin looked at John.

"Go ahead, Professor." John held her head and shoulders close to his chest.

With one, quick pull, the Professor removed the arrow and quickly poured alcohol into the wound. Lessened by weakness, Elisa's response was more of a cry instead of a scream. She slowly looked up at her father and then closed her eyes again.

"Good," the Professor said, as he applied the poultice. "It's bleeding, but not badly."

"Allow me," Pereen said. She quickly knelt by the doctor and washed the young girl's face with a cool, wet rag.

Ever so slowly, Elisa opened her eyes again, looked at Pereen, and then John.

"Father?" she said softly. Raising her right hand, she touched his left check. "Why are you crying?"

The big woodsman smiled down at her. "Just so happy to see you back with us, Elisa."

"Us?" Elisa slowly looked at the people gathered close and smiling down at her.

"Who are all these people, Father and where am I?"

"What do you last remember?" Bo asked.

She raised up slightly, looking at Bo. "My word. You're a Dwarf."

Bo quickly removed his hat as did all the other Dwarves. "Billy Bo Bumpus, My Lady. Please tell us what you last remember."

Elisa pulled grass and leaves from her hair. Looking past the dwarves and into the dark of the woods, she replied, "I was walking home from our neighbor's house on a little trail in the woods when something stung me on my right shoulder. Before I could find out what it was, I got so dizzy I could not stand." She looked up at her father. "I think I fainted but I don't remember hitting the ground."

"As I suspected," Bo grumbled, producing a twenty-inch-long piece of hollowed out cane. He shook it and out fell a black-feathered dart to the grass.

"A stinger," Borack said loudly. "Don't ya touch the thing. It's evil it is."

"It was right here by her when I walked up," Bo added. "She had my number for sure." He looked at the Professor. "One prick with that thing and you would not be able to find your wee pistol."

All the Dwarves laughed loudly, causing smiles to break out on the others. Elisa looked about, slowly smiling herself.

"That's the ticket, My Lady." Fairweather, smiled at Elisa. "Not many folks can say they owe their life to a Dragon. The black witch never figured him into the course of events that fell on her."

Elisa's eyes grew big. "Dragon?" Her voice at a whisper. "Pragamore was here?" She quickly looked at her father. "The Dragon was here?"

John nodded. "That's enough for now. What you need to do is rest."

Pereen looked to Fairweather. "What happened to the witch? The Dragon left so fast, none here could tell what happened."

"One can," Dullbriar said as he walked in from the darkness of the woods with Bitterthorn right behind him.

All eyes were now on Dullbriar, but he just smiled and pointed back with his thumb toward the younger Dwarf who was also smiling.

His smile lasted no more than a half minute before Bo stood, glaring at him. "Out with it, ya field fae afore I sick John on ya."

All laughed at the young dwarf's disappearing smile.

"I will! I will!" He quickly exclaimed. "You all are due an explanation, especially the wounded, young lady. First of all, Dragons know witches, especially Pragamore. Whether the witch knew of the Dragon's presence or not I would have to guess no. The Dragon's blood will, in short time, cast her out. She did, I believe, sense a warm, living being much too close to turn down but Pragamore was smart and pinned the young girl's face down in the grass. The arrow's amethyst head prompted her to make a quick, albeit unwise, decision. Feeling the witch in him, Pragamore knew he had but seconds to flee from everyone before he was found out."

"So…" Helen squinted. "The Dragon now has the witch?"

Bitterthorn slowly shook his head. "I'm powerful sure the evil spirit was within him when he left so fast. High above the clouds he is right now where the air is freezing cold. The blood of the Dragon is slowly, but surely, working its own magic. Ibenus will have to leave the Dragon or slowly be destroyed. Her escape, however, will be short lived for she will not survive the trip to the ground, let alone have the time to search for another host."

"Can we go home now?" Elisa asked.

"Got a better idea," the Professor said as he threw more wood on the fire. "Bo's got a horse trailer and I've got an old MG with a trailer hitch. Why don't we all head to my house in the morning and I'll take you and your father to Phagan's Rift." He paused, looking all about the place. "Where's Entwhistle?"

Donder nodded to his left. "She's at the edge of the woods with Seleene. The wolf won't come close to the fire with all of us here."

Then, as Martin looked toward where Donder had nodded, a

distant sound came riding on the night breeze from the east. It was a sound he was not the least familiar with. The Professor quickly turned to Bo. But he, as well as the others were silent, looking in that same direction.

"What pray tell was that?" Helen asked. "I've heard it somewhere before."

"You certainly have," Long Barr replied. "Remember the Hobuerichs and our adventure in the Yellow Grass with them? What did they send after us that chased us all the way to the big, white oak where the Int was waitin'?"

"Hunting dogs?" the Professor asked.

"Elk hounds," Fairweather grumbled, "and they're runnin' somethin' right now."

"Ohhh-my-God. Those ugly dogs again?" Helen said.

"Shhh," Long Barr hissed.

Everyone immediately stopped talking and looked at Long, and then Donder.

"That's more than one dog," Donder said. His voice low. They're between us and Franklin's Mountain. Their calls are echoing off of them." He looked at Long. "The Hobbs are all dead. They have no keepers now and they're heading south toward the Cut-off area and that lake."

"How many did they have?" Pareen asked.

"Not sure," Long Barr admitted. "Nobody ever got close enough to count 'em. I'll guess between twelve and fifteen maybe. What's more, they're headin' right out of here and deeper into the world of men."

Bo sighed heavily. "At least they're goin' away from us."

Borack looked at Long. "But what if someone connects those Hell Hounds to the Hobs and where they destroyed them. What of those crazy horses they rode—the…"

"Hagstorms," Bo said, "and no more 'what ifs. We've had enough problems for one day. Right now, our biggest problem is gone from us. Pragamore took care of that just as he killed Laphidius Monks way back in Richard's time." He motioned toward the food box. "Bring the whole box and what is left of the meat. There should be potatoes and carrots in there. We'll make a soup for tonight and it'll be enough for all. Perhaps the men of the Cut-off will take care of this Hell Hound thing for us."

Part 6
Return to Phagan's Rift

The next morning, Bo woke to see Fairweather sitting quietly by himself near the remnants of the fire. From the fire, well-wooded and all, it looked as if his brother had been up for a while. Bo slowly looked all about. None of the others were awake and judging from the glow in the east, morning was still young yet.

Bo eased his blanket off and walked to join his brother. Sitting down beside Fairweather, he nudged him with his thumb. "Can't sleep?"

Fairweather slowly shook his head. "How many times in the past have you had the chance ta talk ta one who's known the Wizard Alvis firsthand?"

Bo silently shook his head. "Only in the Tomes I suppose," he finally answered. He looked at his brother. "I think we should go ta Phagan's Rift also. I'd ride in the Professor's smokin' machine for a chance ta see Pragamore one more time."

Fairweather smiled, his eyes still on the fire. "Do ya think he'll remember what a Dwarf is?"

Bo smiled as he looked back to see Bitterthorn sitting up and looking at them.

"We're goin' ta Phagan's Rift from here?" Bitterthorn asked loudly.

"What?" Entwhistle struggled from under her blanket and looked at the two by the fire. "We're goin' with the Professor also?"

Professor Martin propped himself up on his right elbow and rubbed the back of his head where he had rested it on his black bag. He squinted at Entwhistle. "Going where?" he finally got out.

"With us," laughed Helen. "I don't think your MG is going to be big enough."

"Ohhhh…" Martin lay back hard on his black bag. "We could rent something. There's a car rental place not that far from my house."

"We'll pass tha hat," Broderick suggested, rubbing the sleep from his eyes. "I've never seen a Dragon up close, let alone talk ta one."

~ * ~

The next morning, 9:00 a.m. on a beautiful, April day, the Dwarves all sat on the Professor's porch, eying the Grand Caravan he had just rented.

"Got lots o' winders," Broderick noted.

"Smells like leather," Fairweather added.

"Don't smoke either," Bo said.

"Had a dream last night," Dullbriar said with a shot of despair coloring his tone.

Elisa eased up to the screen door, listening to the Dwarves.

"Well..." Fairweather cupped his ears, staring at the young Dwarf. "Gon'na make us guess?"

Dullbriar slowly shook his head. "Dreamed I died in a big, metal coffin—one that always kept movin'. Folks would look in, smile, and then say—"

"Woah!" Elisa, now laughing, stepped out onto the front porch. "I thought Dwarves were fearless. How is it you're going to see a Dragon, yet you're scared of the vehicle that will take you there?"

Fairweather broke out in laughter. "We're warmin' up to it My Lady," he added.

Martin stepped out to join Elisa. "Also, there will be not one weapon taken on this trip. Do you all hear that?"

"Leave 'em here," Fairweather ordered. "We'll trust in those we're goin' with and what we're after as well."

"That's good," the Professor said. "We're leaving in thirty minutes. It'll take about two hours or so to get there. We've got a seven-passenger van, but we're gon'na put ten of us in it. That will be four Dwarves in the rear seat, John, Elisa, and a Dwarf in the middle, and me, Pereen, and Helen in the front. Helen will be our driver."

~ * ~

With only ten miles on the Windamere Road, the Dwarves stopped shying away from the windows and took to looking at everything they passed. Particularly humorous was the young Dullbriar. He seemed to delight in playing with children in the other vehicles as they passed on the divided highway.

About an hour into the trip, Helen glanced back at John, sitting directly behind her. "Did you call the Phagan Farm?"

John nodded. I got Jonathan. His parents left him and Janet the place and moved to Florida when the two got married. There's about two thousand acres of woods and farmland there. I and Elisa work there with Andsell and his granddaughter, Prentis, Johnathan's sister."

At the mention of Andsell, Fairweather quickly stood and pulled himself up behind the middle seat. Cupping his ears, he squinted at John, almost directly in front of him. "Did ya say Andsell just then?"

John looked back, smiling at the old Dwarf. "You heard right, my old friend. This will be a step back in time for some of you. The old Wizard Phagan still lives and is hidden better than the Dragon, Pan's Shadow, I believe."

"Pan's Shadow?" Now Bo was standing alongside of his brother, Fairweather. "Not long ago we were speakin' of Pragamore, not Pandahar. The Pan's been gone for quite a spell."

Elisa smiled at his confused expression. "That's true, Master Dwarf. But Pragamore now looks so much like the Pan, those living in the woods of Dragon's Haunt have taken to calling him Pan's Shadow and sometimes Pan for short. He doesn't seem to mind at all—a compliment I guess."

~ * ~

Thirty minutes later, Helen slowed as they approached a bridge across a beautiful, almost clear, river. Fairweather quickly stood, looked out of the window to his left, and then slowly slipped his hat from his head.

"The Green River," Bo said, causing all the other Dwarves to stand with their hats in their hands also.

"I'm in the dark again," John admitted, noting their solemn attitude.

"Me as well," Helen added. "What happened here?"

"Way before your time, Bright Helen," Broderick said. "One can hardly see it from here, but where this river flows out of Lake Horn, there's a huge, blond stone on its east bank. Pandahar, the Pan, the Dragon of Whitestone, was found there by the Dwarves after he fell in a great battle between the Wizard Richard Alvis and an evil Wizard whose name will not be said. Bo's and Fairweather's father, Brown Tom Bumpus led a group of Dwarves with Richard himself to gather his bones and bring them back to Whitestone Cavern. His ashes were placed under that very stone."

"Now we're goin' ta the east white cliffs of Lake Horn," Fairweather added. "Pragamore resides there even today. I would ask a question of him for sure."

"And what is that?" Bo asked.

"It's somethin' that's been a mystery to me for most of my life. Brown Tom was away from Leachenwood and tendin' his patches of soap root and ginseng when he fell ill. His heart I think. After passing out there, he woke up at the gates of Leachenwood. One moment he wasn't there and the next he was lyin' right at the entranceway."

"Somebody did see it though," Broderick said.

"That would be the watch, old Fisger, but he wasn't himself that day," Bo added.

"He was drunk," Bitterthorn explained, laughing. "Said he saw a huge, russet and yellow colored bird bring 'em in."

"That's not the only question that will be asked this day," Elisa said. Glancing at Helen, she laughed silently.

"Not now," John scolded, his tone firm. "Pragamore will ask that himself."

"Ask what?" Helen glanced back at John, noting Elisa was still grinning.

But John remained strangely quiet as did everyone else, hoping for an answer to Helen's question.

"Well…" Fairweather said finally, looking at John. "Seems you know more than the most of us. What is the Dragon's question?"

"He sees the Wizard Richard in Helen," Elisa replied.

"Elisa!" John scolded again. "You'll frighten the young girl."

Helen's eyes grew big as the van slowed, all but coasting to the right of way. "Now you've got my full attention," she said. Stopping the van, she looked back at John and Elisa. "Please tell me what the Dragon wants."

"And when he saw Helen," Professor Martin asked.

"All right—all right," John conceded. "Perhaps my daughter is right. Helen should be thinkin' on an answer to the question right enough I guess. Pragamore does know of Helen, from the Faes I believe. He's been watchin' her ever since she moved in with her grandfather."

"Go on," Helen prompted.

"He wants you to fly with him," Elisa said, with an eye roll from John.

"What?" Helen stared at the wide-eyed Dwarves.

"Told ya," John grumbled, nudging his daughter.

Helen shoved the shift lever in park, took her foot off the brake, and then looked back at the two again. "I'm not scared. But fly? Did you say fly?"

Elisa nodded. "The Wizard Richard Alvis's blood runs through your veins. I believe he wants to be close to him, through you, for one last time."

"Let's continue," Pereen suggested. "The road to Dragon's Haunt is only a few more miles on the left. It's called Lake View Road."

~ * ~

About twenty minutes later, approximately an hour before noon, Helen slowed as they drew near a paved road leading into the woods on the north side.

"There it is," Bitterthorn said from the middle seats. "How far now?"

"Five miles or so," replied John.

~ * ~

Another twenty minutes put the group in the middle of a pristine forest seemingly untouched by men. Beech trees were so large it would take four men to reach around them. The oaks, some over one hundred feet tall, looked untouched by weather. The canopy was so dense, only ferns and wild grapes and musky dines were allowed to flourish here and there. After a nod from John, Helen turned onto a small, gravel road leading toward a beautiful, white, three-story home with a red barn in the background.

"Stop as the drive passes the porch," instructed John.

As the van pulled closer to the house, all the Dwarves sat up, checking the woods surrounding it. Quickly giving up on that, they glued their eyes on the barn.

"Recon where he is?" Fairweather asked.

"Where who is?" Broderick asked. "The old Wizard Phagan is just as important as the Dragon."

"Do they live here?" Dullbriar asked.

"No," Elisa answered. "They live well past the barn at a place on into the woods near the lake."

"So…Why are we stoppin' here?"

"Stop your talkin'," Fairweather scolded. "We be lucky ta get this far I'd say."

A hush fell over the Dwarves as Helen stopped the van barely ten feet from the east side of the huge, five pillared porch. Facing south, the home sported seven gables above the second floor, each one windowed. The porch, easily twelve feet wide and twenty-five feet long, supported a roof that shaded the windows of the entire second floor. Suddenly losing their curiosity, the Dwarves all settled silently deep in their seats.

"Everybody out!" someone called from the porch.

The feminine voice caused the Dwarves to slowly sit up and look toward the porch. A young woman, in her mid-twenties, stood on the front porch smiling at them. All of five feet and seven inches she was with short, dark brown hair. Her dark eyes mirrored the smile upon her face. Fairweather, with his hat in his hand, was the first out of the van. The other Dwarves, scrambling and tumbling out seemed to be trying for second place. They all quickly gathered up behind the older Dwarf and pulled their hats off also. John and Elisa stepped up beside them with the Professor, Helen, and Pereen at their side.

"I'm Janice Phagan," the young lady said. "John called me last night to say he was leading a little group to visit with us." She smiled at the Dwarves. "I must say, this is a special day for me. My husband is a veterinarian and is on call right now. She looked to John. "Who do you have with you?"

John went on to introduce everyone, but when he got to Helen, Janice stepped toward her, stopping just a short reach away. "I've heard of you Helen Durkin. The Faes are most excited. They are calling you Bright Helen, the Last Wizard of Whitestone."

"Ohhh my," Helen said, forcing a weak smile. "I am certainly no wizard, Ma'am."

Janice smiled. "Old Phagan has spoken to one called Limbisconn. He says there's one most certainly living within you. 'You must let it out.' he says. Pragamore is most excited. He didn't even fly last night. As a matter of fact, he hardly slept at all I am told."

Fairweather stepped forward with his hat crumpled in his

hands. "It's close ta noon, My Lady. Will we see the Dragon today?"

Janice nodded, but her gaze was frozen on Helen. "Does the word Wizard scare you?"

Helen forced another smile. "Not as much as what they say the Dragon wants."

Janice laughed, glancing at John and Elisa. "I would be dead if it were not for Pragamore. He saved my life from what he called a butcher and then carried me here. I remember being in the air with him, but it was all like a dream. He is very careful. So…" She looked about those gathered before her. "Would you have something to eat first, or perhaps go on to the Rift where the Dragon lives?"

Fairweather looked anxiously at John and Pereen, then back to Janice. "Would it be bad form to choose the latter, My Lady?"

"Not at all." Janice looked to Helen. "Leave your van here. I've got two, six passenger electric carts in the back. We'll go there in them."

Janice led the group to the rear of the house. There, under a covered pavilion, were the two carts.

Seeing everyone picking their seats, Janice paused by John. "I would only ask one thing." She looked toward the Dwarves. "If you have weapons, please leave them here."

"We have not, My Lady," Fairweather said. "We were asked to leave them at the Professors' home."

"Good enough," Janice said, as she got in beside John now at the wheel of the first cart. "Take us there, John. I'm sure the Faes have already told Pragamore of Helen's arrival."

~ * ~

So…on they went. Eleven strong and in two vehicles, they passed the new barn and left the hard-paved road for one heavily paved with wood mulch and chips. In just a little more than ten minutes, John slowed the lead cart as they approached another barn. Very large, old, and faded red the cedar was but still stout looking and well maintained with a heavy, metal roof, new windows, and a fieldstone underpinning. On the left and west side of the barn, about thirty yards or so, the white cliffs of Lake Horn. The forest of Dragon's Haunt completely dominated every other side. Slowing the lead cart to a stop, John turned the key off, got out, and then motioned for the second cart to pull alongside and do the same.

Fairweather eased out like a mouse searching a room for the cat. "This is it?" he finally managed. "Such a lonesome place. Don't see a darned thing."

At that very instant, something buzzed through the air from the overhead limbs and struck the old Dwarf on the left cheek.

"Bless my buttons!" he exclaimed, rubbing his cheek briskly. Spinning on his heels, he looked up into the branches of the huge, white oak they were under. "What the devilment was that?" He grumbled as he turned to Janice.

Laughing, she replied, "Watch your words, Master Dwarf. It's what you don't see that can hurt you. There are more eyes on you than you think."

"The Faes of Kiendom watch the Dragon," whispered Pereen.

"It is true then…" Broderick looked up also, "…that they live here also I mean?"

Elisa nodded. "But don't waste your time looking for them. You won't see them unless they trust you."

"Justly said," spoke a young girl as she walked from the barn and into the open. "And they trust very few these days."

Elisa smiled. "This young lady is my husband's sister, Prentis Phagan.

"Pren for short," the dark-haired young girl of nineteen or so said. Dark eyes, dark red lipstick, and pigtails, she stood there at the door with an 'I dare you' smile. Quickly studying the others, her gaze stopped at Helen. "He knows you're here, you know," she added, her tone low. "There's not much you can keep from a Dragon like him. He knew it when you stopped the van on the Green River."

Helen slowly looked back at her grandfather.

"It's time I think," he said with a bit of a smile. "There's your way." He nodded toward the partially open barn door.

"Mine as well," Fairweather said.

The old Dwarf struck a strong and determined pace toward Pren still at the partially open barn door. Seeing his resolve, all the other Dwarves rushed to join in behind him.

"The more the merrier," Pren said with a laugh, pushing the door open wider. "Company like this is a blessing to us any day."

The old Master Dwarf rushed inside as if he owned the place. The others, however, kept a respectable distance so as to see what he might encounter. Helen held back at the door beside Pren with

Pereen and her grandfather looking on. John and Elisa joined them with their smiles all as wide as Pren's.

On past the first stall on the right the Dwarves went and then the second. But when they got to the hay-filled third stall, Fairweather stopped and wheeled to face the other Dwarves.

"He's not here," Fairweather said, with his fists on his hips. "Third stall's full o' hay, the second's empty, and the third's open with a white goat in it.

"Broderick laughed out loud and then nodded at the well in the far, left corner of the open space. "Maybe he's hidin' in the well, Fair."

But as the Dwarves all laughed, there came a strong torrent of warm air into their midst. Swirling up from the first stall, it took dust, hay, and bits of sweet feed with it. All but bumping against her grandfather, Helen backed up from the door, watching the Dwarves bat wildly at the dust and hay.

"Watch the goat," Pren advised. "Snowball knows where the Dragon is."

Noting the nanny was looking toward the back wall, Helen did the same. As she did, the seams in the old cedar boards started to move about, seemingly losing their horizontal lines in places. Little by little, she began to pick out the form of the Dragon.

"Bless my beard." Fairweather's tone was weak as he stepped closer. "Old Alvis's Dragon still lives."

"Amazing isn't it," Pren said. "He started doing this invisibility /chameleon thing about ten years ago. I think it's something to help him survive in his later years."

Pragamore, now fairly visible, nodded to the old Dwarf and then backed away from the goat to the far corner of the stall eying Helen intently.

"Don't move," John warned, looking at Helen. "I don't want him making a new door in the back of his stall."

"My Lady…" Pragamore said, his voice deep and guttural. "You have Richard's aura—white over blue and violet." He raised his head high as though fearful of her.

"Aura?" Helen looked to Pereen as she and the others stepped inside the barn.

Pereen smiled. "That means you are a caring person—protective of others as well as animals. You also have the power to cast off negative energy. That means you can help others as well as call upon those who can assist you."

"Those who can?" Helen's frown was back.

"You're lookin' at one, My Lady," Broderick said. "Another would be the Int."

"But he seems scared of me," Helen whispered.

At that moment, the hinges of the loft doors squeaked, followed by the sound of dry leaves rustling through the stacks of hay above them. The barn's front door closed so hard it made all near jump.

"Stand still and say not a word," Pren instructed. "The Woodland Faes are here. Something's wrong outside."

"Bright Helen…" The voice of the old man was loud and most familiar to her. It seemed to rattle her very ear drums.

She leaned heavily against her grandfather, holding her ears.

"I hear you. What do you want of me?" Helen asked.

"What's she sayin'?" Bo asked as he and the other Dwarves eased closer, eying the Dragon uneasily.

"Didn't hear a thing," John said, with the others shaking their heads also.

The voice of the Int spoke again. "You and yours must stay inside for the moment. The Faes will tell you when it's safe."

"I heard it," spoke someone directly above Helen.

Looking to the rafters in the open part of the loft floor, Helen could readily see a good number of little people right above her. Dressed in the colors of spring, and of many different ages, all were sitting except for one. All of a foot tall or so, the little lady was dressed entirely of leaf green.

"It is the Int, you know," she said, smiling at Helen. "You're green as grass juice, but you'll get used to him. He said to stay inside with us. The Dryads are in every tree close to the barn. Somethin's up and there's gon'na be some kind of fight I think." She quickly flew to Pren's left shoulder, still watching Helen closely.

"Who are you?" Helen asked.

"Rosebud," Pren answered, laughing.

"Pren!" The little fae grabbed Pren's left ear and twisted it.

"Ok—Ok," Pren squealed wincing. "We're all friends here. Besides, Helen will need a 'Go To' from the Woodlands. You would be perfect. You served Richard as well."

"Bless me," Bo said weakly. The Tomes list two Faes as the old wizard's Go To's."

"Lilly Ann," Rosebud said. "She's following the Hounds for the Dryads. They won't leave the Int."

Then, from the outside, there came the sound of wind and limbs rubbing against one another. So intense it was, it shook the doors and windows of the old barn and rattled its tin roof. In the midst of the wind, were the shrill sounds of the hounds—some growling and others barking in fright. Helen eased from her grandfather and peeked out of the window just right of the double doors. By that time, the sound was growing weaker. She could see, however, a dark and spinning cloud. Low over the trees to the southeast it was but still very close. Slowly rotating like some weird thunderhead, it brushed the tops of the huge oaks as it moved away from the barn.

"It's gone," Rosebud said. "It took the devil dogs with it also."

"Did it kill them?" Dullbriar asked. The young dwarf edged closer to Pren, eying the little Woodland Fae.

She quickly shook her head. "Don't think so. The Int seldom has anything killed."

"Among the last of the Hobuerich's existence," the Dragon said, still looking at Helen intently.

Helen looked to the Dragon. "One of ours has a question. His father fell ill while in the woods and something brought him to Leachenwood."

Fairweather slowly stepped forward. Holding his hat in his hand, he looked anxiously at the Dragon.

Pragamore looked straight at Fairweather. "That would be Brown Tom. I would be that 'something'."

"I knew it!" Fairweather exclaimed. "My father wasn't lyin' after all."

Helen looked at the Dragon again. "But that's not your question is it?"

"No, My Lady," Pragamore said, gently rubbing the white goat. "Your aura is very close to the Wizard Alvis. You must visit Phagan right now." He nodded toward what looked to be two slanted doors near the far, left corner of the barn's open space.

"Take them to the Grandfather," Janice said to Pren. "It's time for his lunch; John and I will bring it from the main house. He would love the company, especially since he'll have a chance to talk to Helen."

Pren nodded. "This way," she said as she walked to the doors just left of the well. Opening them, she looked back at the others. "The stairs are made of stone. They are not steep. Hold to one of the rails on either side of the stairway."

"You first," Helen said, looking at Pren.

Laughing, Pren led the way down the five-foot-wide stairway. Although dimly lit, she could see past Pren and on to a heavy look-ing wooden door at their end. Pren stopped at the doorway and slowly opened it. Light shot inside the stairway accompanied by a most shrill whistle from somewhere inside the room on the other side.

"What in tarnation was that?" Bo asked, now looking past those in front of him and toward the open door.

"It's Apple," Pren said with a laugh. "He's a big, green and white bird."

"A McCaw," the person holding the door open for them said.

Helen looked past Pren to see an old, white-haired man smiling back at her. His bright, blue eyes were as distracting as the scar down the left side of his face. He had on a tawny, brown robe held close to his waist by a solid, white rope.

"Well—well," he said, reaching for Helen's hand. "I finally get to meet you."

The old fellow smiled at the Dwarves as they seemed to be distracted by something fluttering about the rafters above the lights of the room.

"To your perch, Apple." Pren pointed to the far, left corner of the huge room.

Following the red and green flash from above the lights, Helen watched the huge bird glide across a spacious room. Over half the size of a basketball court it seemed and ended at four, huge sets of windows overlooking the lake.

"There's a table set up at the windows if you please," the old fellow said. "I'm Andsell Phagan. Company's as scarce as hen's teeth around here."

The Dwarves eyed the work benches and storage shelves on each side of the entrance to the room. They were labeled various oils, herbs, stones, roots, and powders. As they entered the well-lit area of the room, Helen could see the one called the Grandfather was indeed well up in his years. Although his hair was remarkably thin, there was still much stability in his step and life in his words and expression. Then, she realized she was looking straight at him.

"Curious?" he asked, now looking directly at her.

She immediately jumped, pulling her stare away from his scar. "I'm—sooo—sorry," she said. "I didn't want to appear rude in any way."

Andsell smiled, glancing at the others. All were very quiet, awaiting the next comment.

"No harm, young one," he added, laughing. "Truth be told, I'm just as curious about you."

"How did you…" Helen slowly moved her fingertips to the left side of her face.

"Ohhh, the scar." His smile widened. "When fighting a man on a dragon, it would be prudent to keep an eye on the dragon also. I was a bit older than you, but young none-the-less. It was a life-changing moment for me I would say." He paused, looking deep into her eyes. "You are approaching one of those moments right now. I would suggest you embrace it. But that's just me."

"Embrace what?" Helen's voice was weak.

Andsell smiled again as he paused at the table and gestured for them to take a seat. He again looked at Helen. "When you met Pragamore did he act strangely toward you?"

"Well…" Helen paused, glancing at Pren. "He acted kind of fearful of me, I think."

"Cautious," Andsell corrected. "He knew if you touched him, something would happen to you." His smile widened. "There's your moment, Helen Durkin. It has to be your decision to connect with the past."

"Something would happen to me?" Helen paused, staring unconsciously at the one everyone called The Old Wizard.

"It's nare a bad thing, My Lady," Fairweather said as he eased from the rest, stopping at Andsell's side. "Either Whitestone dies here or it lives on in you once you touch the dragon." Realizing he might have spoken out of turn, he glanced at Andsell, looked down, and then backed up a bit.

Holding the smile, Andsell replied, "Well said, Master Dwarf. It certainly would not harm you. But, let us away for right now. It's several hours before dark comes, but I don't believe Pragamore will fly tonight without you. Right now, I think our food has arrived."

The heavy, wooden door swung open and in stepped Janice with a big, wicker basket covered with a white cloth. Right behind her was John carrying a huge, roasting pot.

"Hungry?" Janice asked as she placed the basket upon the table. "Right here," she said to John, pointing beside the basket.

John placed the pot upon a short, metal stand and turned to Helen. "Have ya made a decision, Lass?"

"I..." Helen paused, looking at Billy Bo Bumpus. "What should I do?"

Bo shrugged. "This must be your decision, Lass. You've made many friends this year. If you connect with Pragamore, you will make a great many more I think. If you choose to do so, Andsell will guide and advise you I'm sure. You must then stay here for three months or so."

Helen looked to her grandfather. "I'll do it."

A loud cheer went up from the Dwarves with all others smiling and applauding.

~ * ~

Later that evening, just after dusk, Helen stood from the couch and looked toward the door leading to the stairway to the barn. "Do you think he's still up there?" she asked, almost as a spoken thought.

Andsell smiled, almost laughing. "Absolutely, My Lady. After all, you were the main reason he flew anyway."

"He watched me?" Helen's eyes narrowed.

Fairweather nodded. "Watched over you, My Lady. Almost a year ago, Bo was told there was someone of note staying at the Professor's home. She, a young lady, should be watched and protected."

"Twas a Fae it was who brought the word," Bo explained. "When a Fae brings you a message it is usually sent by another much greater." He shrugged, looking at Andsell. "I got a little too close that first day and what with Helen getting lost and then tracked by the wolf Seleene. Well, here we are."

Pereen stood, looking at Helen. "Go on, Bright Helen. We'll be up there at your side."

Helen slowly stood, watching Pren open the stairway door. "I'll lead the way," Pren said softly.

Helen followed Pren, with John, Pereen, and her grandfather right behind her. The Dwarves, all quiet and in single file, followed. Andsell, however, opted not to tackle the stairs for the moment. Gaining the head of the stairs, Helen followed Pren into the barn and paused by the well. Ten oil lanterns had been lit and hung from hooks on the rafters and walls. As the Dwarves entered, Helen slowly stepped toward the center of the barn, looking toward the far stall on the left. Standing erect, Pragamore's yellow eyes reflected the yellow flames in the lanterns. Helen paused, almost halfway.

"Lass..." Bo stepped to her side and whispered, "He considers you a friend. Sadden him it would to behold fear in your eyes."

Helen smiled, and then slowly walked toward the dragon. Seeing her getting close, Snowball backed between Pragamore's fore hands and eyed her cautiously. "Please be patient with me, Pragamore. The fear that is within me is not of you, but of what comes next."

"Well put, My Lady," the dragon said. "But the 'what comes next' has done me no harm these past, many years."

Seeing her getting closer, Pragamore backed well into the stall. His head held high as if still apprehensive.

Helen stopped immediately. "Do you fear me?"

Pragamore slowly shook his head. "The touch must be deliberate, My Lady."

Helen smiled, holding her right hand out toward him, palm up. "I have made an effort. Would you meet me halfway?"

Pragamore looked straight at John, who by this time, had eased up to Helen's left side.

"As she said," John said. "She's offering a pact with you."

Then, with a step forward, Pragamore lowered his head and eased toward Helen's outstretched hand. As they touched, the Dragon shut his eyes. Helen, however, was blinded by a bright, white light. The blurry flash of a huge riven signaled the beginning of countless scenes. A young man in a large, dimly lit cavern, flying over countless lakes and forests, and getting struck by a strange bolt of energy from a strange, old woman, were just a few. But when she beheld the figure of a man who seemed to glow with a light emitted from inside his own body, the visions stopped.

"Helen? Helen?"

The words seemed to echo as if in a vast cave. Helen slowly opened her eyes to find herself lying upon the floor in John's arms.

"Are you all right, My Lady?" came the question spoken by someone quite close. The voice, low and guttural, was now one she was very familiar with—the Dragon Pragamore.

Helen slowly sat up, looking at the blurry figures gathered close around her. "Fine, I believe," she managed, rubbing her eyes. She looked up at the Dragon. "We have much to talk about, Pragamore. I have seen people and places I am not the least familiar with and…"

Her voice trailed off, searching for words.

"And, My Lady?" the Dragon prompted.

"I saw a glowing person. I know not who it was, but he seemed to glow with many colors as it were."

"It's part of the 'Second Sight', My Lady," Pragamore explained. It's called 'The Dark See'."

Helen slowly nodded. "Am I allowed to know what that is?"

The dragon eased closer, watching her expression. There was no fear in her eyes. "Come fly with me."

About the Author

M.R. Williamson was born on Aprill 22, 1945, to a lower middle-class family on the outskirts of Memphis, TN. At that time, the 'baby boomers' were just budding into existence. His father's parents were a good part Native American of the Pawnee persuasion. They belonged to the Wolf-Cipi clan. His wife, Connie, has spent many long hours studying this genealogical question mark. Some of her studies have pointed her to Kansas with the names Two Shirts, Two Chiefs, Williamsons, and Russells.

Although his mother, Dorothy, was English and Scottish, his father, Russell, held fast to his Native American traits. The love of the woods, freedom, and nature were some of his strongest. These were surpassed only by the love he held for his family. M. R. has one brother, Ronald, and two sisters, Sandra and Tammy. Through his guidance, they were taught to love and respect every aspect of life. This was especially true for the 'little' ones of the wild. Because of this, and through his wife's understanding, M. R. has spent countless hours in the woods and on the waters. He has seen a number of things that would be, at least for him, hard to explain. He has always held a deep interest in the world of faeries and the mystical unknown. Some would call this fantasy or fiction, but there are those who would not.

As for M. R., he's never seen a dragon, nor had the pleasure of swapping stories with the fae people. He has, however, talked to a few rational people who have…according to them. His younger sister, Tammy, and her husband, Terry Barr, have also been severely bitten by this mythical bug. Terry, being a Tolkien expert, and an accomplished artist, has succeeded in fanning the flames of M. R.'s unyielding curiosity.

More Books by M. R. Williamson from WolfSinger Publications

The Moleskin Cap - M. R. Williamson

Helen is trying to get over the recent loss of her mother. Seeing the struggle, her father sends her to live with her grandparents.

Now among the forests her mother loved, Helen connects with her mother's hobby, photography. With her mother's first camera, an old Nikon, she snaps a shadowy figure in the early-morning shade of a fir tree.

The resulting friendship not only pulls her from the destructive depression she was sinking into, but leads Helen into a world of magic and adventure and gives her a new purpose in life and a new reason to live.

Get ready for more adventures with these fantasy books from WolfSinger Publications.

Maya, Resurrected – Kimberly Todd Wade

859 A.D. Yohl Ik'nal ("Heart of the Wind Place") is alone with her two starving children on their drought-stricken farm. Her husband and two grown sons have been drafted to fight in a distant war. Will they ever return? Yohl can't afford to wait. Her hungry children must be fed. It's time to dig up Yohl's past, for her mother was a princess, her grandfather a king. She still has relatives amongst the Maya royalty. They are her best hope for salvation.

Follow Yohl and her children as they travel Maya causeways, highways of the ancient world, through ravaged jungle and depressed homesteads to the capital city, itself on the verge of economic collapse.

Can the religious spectacle of human sacrifice provoke the Gods' beneficence? If the Maya ceremonies and myths fail, Yohl has recourse to the older, deeper traditions of the forest people.

She'll do whatever necessary to survive.

Seventh Daughter – Ronnie Seagren

Some people are destined from birth to do great things.

Gil Orlov is born in the shadow of totality of a solar eclipse, the seventh daughter of a seventh daughter. She is the culmination of a carefully planned genealogy begun by her great-grandmother. Gil's purpose, the goal of her family—defeating a Vision of the world in flames, reduced to a lifeless cinder.

But the power she should have is muted or lacking. Gil and her six sisters begin an arduous journey to a place of power high in the Peruvian Andes known as Killichaka—the Bridge to the Moon. They must make it to this ancient temple in time to complete a ritual during the totality of the 1937 solar eclipse. If they are successful, Gil's powers should be restored—giving her the ability to prevent the global disaster her ancestors warned of.

To succeed they must first survive the journey and locate

Killichaka. Against them is the environment, the elements, their own doubts and fears as well as the 'Other' and a force that would gleefully see the world fall into chaos—an entity known as Supay.

Small-g City – S.D. Matley

Seattle is on the brink of disaster, but nobody knows it! Nobody except Ralph, a "small-g" god from Olympus, Inc.

Ralph suffers from extreme job burn-out, and no wonder—his job is to reinforce Seattle's notorious raised highway, the Alaskan Way Viaduct, by disbursing his molecules throughout the unstable and hazardous structure.

But Ralph's molecules are feeling the pull of reconstitution. Will he survive one more agonizing rush hour without resuming his humanoid form and emerging from the viaduct, sending thousands of commuters to their deaths? And what about the familiar shadow hovering over him? If Zeus (Olympus, Inc. CEO and the Biggest of Big-G Gods) is spying on him, all Tartarus is sure to break loose!

Big-G City – S.D. Matley

Veronica Zeta, youngest child of Zeus and Hera, is at last CEO of the immortal owned and operated corporation, Olympus, Inc. The biggest project on her agenda is creating world peace, but first she must depose her bloodthirsty brother Ares, God of War. To do so, she must deploy a supernatural force called The Power, which can demand a terrible price.

Zeus, former CEO and Ex-Lord of the Universe, struggles with identity issues after his retirement. The bright spot in his life is babysitting his toddler granddaughter, but his marriage with Hera is foundering and he longs for someone to confide in.

Hera's new campaign, a mortal lifestyle series of books and seminars called Marvelous Marriage, is a huge success. The face of this project, small-g goddess Candy Smith, has become a media celebrity. Hera, Goddess of Marriage, revels in the market share she's stealing from the "adult" industries owned by her rival, Aphrodite.

But Aphrodite, Goddess of Love, is ready to fight back! Employing a photo-shopped tabloid cover photo and a box of enchanted chocolates, she disrupts the personal life of Candy Smith and goads Hera into executing her own sabotage plan.

The lives of these Olympians collide when Veronica succeeds in deposing Ares, and pays for deploying a large dose The Power with blindness, anguish and, possibly, death. But how can an immortal die? The answer lies in an old family secret, daringly unearthed by Zeus in the eleventh hour.

Find out more about these and our other books at
www.wolfsingerpubs.com